MR STINK

David Walliams

Illustrated by Quentin Blake

GALAXY
PLUS

First published 2009 by
HarperCollins Children's Books,
a division of
HarperCollins Publishers Ltd
This Large Print edition published 2011 by
AudioGO Ltd
by arrangement with
HarperCollins Publishers Ltd

ISBN: 978 1405 664516

British Library Cataloguing in Publication Data available

Printed and bound in Great Britain by
TJ International Ltd

For my mum Kathleen,
the kindest person I have ever met.

Thank yous:

Once again Quentin Blake has honoured my writing with his sublime illustrations, and to him I am enormously grateful. I still can't quite believe I have collaborated with him, as he is such a legend. Other people who I would like to thank are Mario Santos and Ann-Janine Murtagh at HarperCollins for believing in me once again. Nick Lake, my editor, deserves a big thank you for making me work so hard and taking me out for tea and cakes. The copy editor Alex Antscherl, cover designer James Annal and text designer Elorine Grant have all done magnificent jobs on this too. Also thank you to all the people at HarperCollins who work so diligently to promote and distribute the book, particularly Sam White. My literary agent Paul Stevens at Independent is a very nice man too, and dealt brilliantly with all the important contractual things that my brain cannot process.

*   *   *

Finally I would also like to thank all the people who wrote to me to say they enjoyed my first book, *The Boy in the Dress*, particularly the children. It is very touching when someone takes the time to write a letter, and greatly encouraged me when working on *Mr Stink*. I hope it doesn't disappoint.

SCRATCH 'N' SNIFF

Mr Stink stank. He also stunk. And if it is correct English to say he stinked, then he stinked as well. He was the stinkiest stinky stinker who ever lived.

A stink is the worst type of smell. A stink is worse than a stench. And a stench is worse than a pong. And a pong is worse than a whiff. And a whiff can be enough to make your nose wrinkle.

It wasn't Mr Stink's fault that he stank. He was a tramp, after all. He didn't have a home and so he never had the opportunity to have a proper wash like you and me. After a while the smell just got worse and worse. Here is a picture of Mr Stink.

He is quite a snappy dresser in his bow-tie and tweed jacket, isn't he? But don't be fooled. The illustration doesn't do justice to the smell. This could be a scratch 'n' sniff book, but the smell would be so bad you would have to put it in the bin. And then bury the bin. Very deep underground.

That's his little black dog with him, the Duchess. The Duchess wasn't any particular breed of dog, she was just a dog. She smelt too, but not as bad as Mr Stink. Nothing in the world really smelt as bad as him. Except his beard. His beard was full of old bits of egg and sausage and cheese that had fallen out of his mouth years before. It had never, ever been shampooed so it had its own special stink, even worse than his main one.

One morning, Mr Stink simply appeared in the town and took up residence on an old wooden bench. No one knew where he had come from, or where he might be going. The town folk were mostly nice to him. They sometimes dropped a few coins at his feet, before rushing off with their eyes watering. But no one was really *friendly* towards him. No one stopped for a chat.

At least, not till the day that a little girl finally plucked up the courage to speak to him—and that's where our story begins.

'Hello,' said the girl, her voice trembling a little with nerves. The girl was called Chloe. She was only twelve and she had never spoken to a tramp before. Her mother had forbidden her to speak to 'such creatures'. Mother even disapproved of her daughter talking to kids from the local council estate. But Chloe didn't think Mr Stink *was* a creature. She thought he was a man who looked

2

like he had a very interesting story to tell—and if there was one thing Chloe loved, it was stories.

Every day she would pass him and his dog in her parents' car on the way to her posh private school. Whether in sunshine or snow, he was always sitting on the same bench with his dog by his feet. As she luxuriated on the leather of the back seat with her poisonous little sister Annabelle, Chloe would look out of the window at him and wonder.

Millions of thoughts and questions would swim through her head. Who was he? Why did he live on the streets? Had he ever had a home? What did his dog eat? Did he have any friends or family? If so, did they know he was homeless?

Where did he go at Christmas? If you wanted to write him a letter, what address would you put on the envelope? 'The bench, you know the one—round the corner from the bus stop'? When was the last time he'd had a bath? And could his name *really* be Mr Stink?

Chloe was the kind of girl who loved being alone with her thoughts. Often she would sit on her bed and make up stories about Mr Stink. Sitting on her own in her room, she would come up with all kinds of fantastical tales. Maybe Mr Stink was a heroic old sailor who had won dozens of medals for bravery, but had found it impossible to adapt to life on dry land? Or perhaps he was a world-famous opera singer who one night, upon hitting the top note in an aria at the Royal Opera House in London, lost his voice and could never sing again? Or maybe he was really a Russian secret agent who had put on an elaborate tramp disguise to spy on the people of the town?

Chloe didn't know anything about Mr Stink. But

3

what she did know, on that day when she stopped to talk to him for the first time, was that he looked like he needed the five-pound note she was holding *much* more than she did.

He seemed lonely too, not just alone, but lonely in his soul. That made Chloe sad. She knew full well what it was like to feel lonely. Chloe didn't like school very much. Mother had insisted on sending her to a posh all-girls secondary school, and she hadn't made any friends there. Chloe didn't like being at home much either. Wherever she was she had the feeling that she didn't quite fit in.

What's more, it was Chloe's least favourite time of year. Christmas. Everyone is supposed to love Christmas, especially children. But Chloe hated it. She hated the tinsel, she hated the crackers, she hated the carols, she hated having to watch the Queen's speech, she hated the mince pies, she hated that it never really snowed like it's supposed to, she hated sitting down with her family to a long, long dinner, and most of all, she hated how she had to pretend to be happy just because it was December 25th.

'What can I do for you, young lady?' said Mr Stink. His voice was unexpectedly posh. As no one had ever stopped to talk to him before, he stared slightly suspiciously at this plump little girl. Chloe was suddenly a bit frightened. Maybe it wasn't such a good idea to talk to the old tramp after all. She had been working up to this moment for weeks, months even. This wasn't how it had all played out in her head.

To make matters worse, Chloe had to stop breathing through her nose. The smell was starting to get to her. It was like a living thing, creeping its way up her nostrils and burning the back of her throat.

'Erm, well, sorry to bother you . . .'

'Yes?' said Mr Stink, a little impatiently. Chloe was taken aback. Why was he in such a hurry? He *always* sat on his bench. It wasn't like he suddenly needed to go somewhere else.

At that moment the Duchess started barking at her. Chloe felt even more scared. Sensing this, Mr Stink pulled the Duchess's lead, which was really just a bit of old rope, to encourage her to be quiet.

'Well,' Chloe went on nervously, 'my auntie sent me five pounds to buy myself a Christmas present. But I don't really need anything so I thought I would give it to you.'

Mr Stink smiled. Chloe smiled too. For a moment it looked as if he was going to accept Chloe's offer, then he looked down at the pavement.

'Thank you,' he said. 'Unimaginable kindness, but I can't take it, sorry.'

Chloe was confused. 'Why ever not?' she asked.

'You are but a child. Five pounds? It's too, too generous.'

'I just thought—'

'It's really kind of you, but I'm afraid I can't accept. Tell me, how old are you, young lady? Ten?'

'TWELVE!' said Chloe loudly. She was a little short for her age, but liked to think she was grown-up in lots of other ways. 'I'm twelve. Thirteen on January the ninth!'

'Sorry, you're twelve. Nearly thirteen. Go and buy yourself one of those new musical stereo discs. Don't you worry about an old vagabond like me.' He smiled. There was a real twinkle in his eye when he smiled.

'If it's not too rude,' said Chloe, 'can I ask you a question?'

'Yes, of course you can.'

'Well, I would love to know: why do you live on a bench and not in a house like me?'

Mr Stink shuffled slightly and looked anxious. 'It's a long story, my dear,' he said. 'Maybe I will tell you another day.'

Chloe was disappointed. She wasn't sure there would *be* another day. If her mother found out that she was even talking to this man, let alone offering him money, she would do her nut.

'Well, sorry for bothering you,' said Chloe. 'Have a lovely day.' As the words came out she cringed. What a stupid thing to say! How could he possibly have a lovely day? He was a smelly old tramp, and the sky was growing gloomy with black clouds. She took a few paces up the street, feeling embarrassed.

'What's that on your back, child?' called out Mr Stink.

'What's what on my back?' asked Chloe, trying to look over her shoulder. She reached round and tore a piece of paper from her blazer. She peered at it.

Written on the piece of paper, in thick black letters, was a single word.

LOSER!

Chloe felt her stomach twist with humiliation. Rosamund must have sellotaped it to her when she left school. Rosamund was the head girl of the cool gang. She was always bullying Chloe, picking on her for eating too many sweets, or for being poorer than the other girls at school, or for being the girl neither team ever wanted on their side in hockey matches. As Chloe had left school today Rosamund patted her on the back several times, saying 'Merry Christmas', while all the other girls laughed. Now Chloe knew why. Mr Stink rose creakily from his bench and took the paper from Chloe's hands.

'I can't believe I've been going round with that on my back all afternoon,' said Chloe. Embarrassed to feel tears welling up, she looked away, blinking into the sunlight.

'What is it, child?' asked Mr Stink, kindly.

Chloe sniffed. 'Well,' she said, 'it's true, isn't it? I really am a loser.'

Mr Stink bent down to look at her. 'No,' he said, authoritatively. 'You're not a loser. The real loser

is the person who stuck it to you in the first place.'

Chloe tried to believe him, but couldn't quite. For as long as she could remember she had felt like a loser. Maybe Rosamund and all those other girls in her gang were right.

'There's only one place for this,' said Mr Stink. He screwed up the piece of paper and, like a professional cricketer, expertly bowled it into the bin. Chloe clocked this and her imagination instantly started whirring; had he once been captain of the England cricket team?

Mr Stink brushed his hands together. 'Good riddance to bad rubbish,' he said.

'Thanks,' murmured Chloe.

'Not at all,' said Mr Stink. 'You mustn't let bullies get you down.'

'I'll try,' said Chloe. 'Nice to meet you Mr . . . um . . .' she began. Everyone called him Mr Stink, but she didn't know if he knew that. It felt rude to say it to his face.

'Stink,' he said. 'They call me Mr Stink.'

'Oh. Nice to meet you, Mr Stink. I'm Chloe.'

'Hello, Chloe,' said Mr Stink.

'You know, Mr Stink,' said Chloe, 'I still might

go the shops. Do you need anything? Like a bar of soap or something?'

'Thank you, my dear,' he replied. 'But I have no use for soap. You see, I had a bath only last year. But I would *love* some sausages. I do adore a nice meaty sausage . . .'

2

ICY SILENCE

'Mother?' said Annabelle.

Mother finished chewing her food completely, then swallowed it, before finally replying.

'Yes, my darling child?'

'Chloe just took one of her sausages off her plate and hid it in her napkin.'

It was Saturday evening, and the Crumb family sat at the dining room table, missing *Strictly Come Dancing* and *The X-Factor* as they ate their dinner. Mother had banned watching television and eating at the same time. She had decided that it was 'awfully common'. Instead the family had to sit in icy silence and eat their dinner staring at the walls. Or sometimes Mother would choose a subject for discussion, normally what she would do if she ran the country. That was her absolute favourite. Mother had given up running a beauty salon to stand for Parliament, and had no doubt in her mind that one day she would be Prime Minister.

Mother had named the white Persian family cat Elizabeth, after the Queen. She was obsessed with Being Posh. There was a downstairs loo that was kept locked for 'very important guests', as if a member of the royal family was going to swing by for a waz. There was a china tea set in the cupboard that was 'for best', and had never once been used. Mother even sprayed air freshener in the garden. Mother would never go out, and not even answer the door, unless immaculately groomed, with her beloved pearls around her neck and her hair made stiff with enough hairspray to create its own hole in the ozone layer. She was so used to turning up her nose at everybody and everything, it was in danger of staying that way. Here's a picture of her.

My word, she looks posh, doesn't she?

Unsurprisingly Father, or Dad as he preferred to be called when Mother wasn't around, opted for a quiet life and usually didn't speak unless spoken to. He was a big powerful man, but his wife made him feel small inside. Dad was only forty, but he was already going bald and starting to stoop. He worked long hours at a car factory on the edge of the town.

'Did you hide a sausage in your napkin, Chloe?' demanded Mother.

'You are always trying to get me into trouble!'

snapped Chloe.

This was true. Annabelle was two years younger than Chloe, and one of those children adults think are perfect, but other children don't like because they are snotty little goody-goodies. Annabelle loved getting Chloe into trouble. She would lie on her bed in her bright pink room upstairs and roll around crying, shouting 'CHLOE, GET OFF ME! YOU ARE HURTING ME!' even though Chloe was quietly writing away in her room next door. You *could* say that Annabelle was evil. She was certainly evil to her older sister.

'Oh, sorry Mother, it just slipped into my lap,' said Chloe guiltily. Her plan had been to smuggle the sausage out for Mr Stink. She had been thinking about him all evening, imagining him shivering out there in the cold dark December night as they sat in the warm, eating away.

'Well then Chloe, unroll it from your napkin and put it back on your plate,' ordered Mother. 'I am so ashamed that we are even eating sausages for dinner. I gave your father strict instructions to dispatch himself to the supermarket and purchase four wild sea-bass fillets. And he comes home with a packet of sausages. If anyone called around and saw us eating food like this it would be hideously embarrassing. They'd think we were savages!'

'I am sorry, my darling wife,' protested Dad. 'They were all out of wild sea-bass fillets.' He gave Chloe the tiniest wink as he said this, confirming her suspicion that he had deliberately disobeyed Mother's orders. Chloe smiled at him discreetly. She and her dad both loved sausages and lots of other food that Mother didn't approve of, like burgers, fish-fingers, fizzy drinks, and especially

13

Mr Whippy ice-cream ('the devil's spume', Mother called it). 'I have never eaten anything from a van,' she would say. 'I'd rather die.'

'Right now, all hands on deck as we clear up,' said Mother when they had finished eating. 'Annabelle, my precious angel, you clear the table, Chloe, you can wash up and Husband, you can dry.' When she said 'all hands on deck', what she really meant was everybody's hands except hers. As the rest of the family all went about their duties Mother reclined on the sofa and started unwrapping a wafer-thin chocolate mint. She allowed herself one chocolate mint a day. She nibbled so infuriatingly slowly she made each one last an hour.

'One of my Bendicks luxury chocolate mints has gone walkies again!' she called out.

Annabelle shot Chloe an accusing look before returning to the dining room to collect some more plates. 'I bet it was you, fatty!' she hissed.

'Be nice, Annabelle,' chided Dad.

Chloe felt guilty, even though it wasn't her who had been scoffing her mother's chocolates. She and Dad assumed their familiar positions at the sink.

'Chloe, why were you trying to hide one of your sausages?' he asked. 'If you didn't like it, you could have just said.'

'I wasn't trying to hide it, Dad.'

'Then what were you doing with it?'

Suddenly Annabelle appeared with another stack of dirty plates and the pair fell silent. They waited a moment until she had gone.

'Well, Dad, you know that tramp who always sits on the same bench every—'

14

'Mr Stink?'

'Yes. Well, I thought his dog looked hungry and I wanted to bring her a sausage or two.'

It was a lie, but not a big one.

'Well, I suppose there isn't any harm in giving his poor dog a bit of food,' said Dad. 'Just this once though, you understand?'

'But—'

'Just this once, Chloe. Or Mr Stink will expect you to feed his dog every day. Now, I hid another packet of sausages behind the crème fraîche, whatever that is. I'll cook them up for you before your mother gets up tomorrow morning and you can give them—'

'WHAT ARE YOU TWO CONSPIRING ABOUT?' demanded Mother from the sitting room.

'Oh, erm, we were just debating which of the Queen's four children we most admire,' said Dad. 'I am putting forward Anne for her equestrian skills, though Chloe is making a strong case for Prince Charles and his unrivalled range of organic biscuits.'

'Very good. Carry on!' boomed the voice from next door.

Dad smiled at Chloe cheekily.

3

THE WANDERER

Mr Stink ate the sausages in an unexpectedly elegant manner. First he took out a little linen napkin and tucked it under his chin. Next he took an antique silver knife and fork out of his breast pocket. Finally he produced a dirty gold-rimmed china plate, which he gave to the Duchess to lick clean before he set down the sausages neatly upon it.

Chloe stared at his cutlery and plate. This seemed like another clue to his past. Had he perhaps been a gentleman thief who crept into country houses at midnight and made off with the family silver?

'Do you have any more sausages?' asked Mr Stink, his mouth still full of sausage.

'No, just those eight I'm afraid,' replied Chloe.

She stood at a safe distance from the tramp, so that her eyes wouldn't start weeping at the smell. The Duchess looked up at Mr Stink as he ate the sausages, with a heartbreaking longing that suggested that all love and all beauty was contained in those tubes of meat.

'There you go, Duchess,' said Mr Stink, slowly lowering half a sausage into his dog's mouth. The Duchess was so hungry she didn't even chew; instead she swallowed it in half a millisecond before returning to her expression of sausage-longing. Had any man or beast ever eaten a sausage so quickly? Chloe was half-expecting a gentleman in a blazer and slacks with a clipboard and stopwatch to appear and declare that the little black dog had set a new sausage-eating international world record!

'So, young Chloe, is everything fine at home?' asked Mr Stink, as he let the Duchess lick his fingers clean of any remnants of sausage juice.

'I'm sorry?' replied a befuddled Chloe.

'I asked if everything was fine at home. If things were tickety-boo I am not sure you would be spending your Sunday talking to an old vagabond like me.'

'Vagabond?'

'I don't like the word "tramp". It makes you think of someone who smells.'

Chloe tried to conceal her surprise. Even the Duchess looked puzzled and she didn't speak English, only Dog.

'I prefer vagabond, or wanderer,' continued Mr Stink.

The way he put it, thought Chloe, it sounded almost poetic. Especially 'wanderer'. She would love to be a wanderer. She would wander all around the world if she could. Not stay in this boring little town where nothing happened that hadn't happened the day before.

'There's nothing wrong at home. Everything is fine,' said Chloe adamantly.

'Are you *sure*?' enquired Mr Stink, with the wisdom some people have that cuts right through you like a knife through butter.

Things were, in fact, not at all fine at home for Chloe. She was often ignored. Her mother doted on Annabelle—probably because her youngest daughter was like a miniature version of her. Every

17

inch of every wall in the house was covered with celebrations of Annabelle's infinite achievements.

Photographs of her standing smugly on winner's podiums, certificates bearing her name emblazoned in italic gold, trophies and statuettes and medals engraved with 'winner', 'first place' or 'little creep'. (I made up that last one.)

The more Annabelle achieved, the more Chloe felt like a failure. Her parents spent most of their lives providing a chauffeur service for Annabelle's out of school activities. Her schedule was exhausting even to *look* at.

18

Monday
5am   Swimming training
6am   Clarinet lesson
7am   Dance lesson, tap and contemporary
         jazz
8am   Dance lesson, ballet
9am to 4pm School
4pm   Drama lesson, improvisation and
         movement
5pm   Piano lesson
6pm   Brownies
7pm   Girls' Brigade
8pm   Javelin practice

Tuesday
4am   Violin lesson
5am   Stilt-walking practice
6am   Chess Society
7am   Learning Japanese
8am   Flower-arranging class
9am to 4pm School
4pm   Creative writing workshop
5pm   Porcelain frog painting class
6pm   Harp practice
7pm   Watercolour painting class
8pm   Dance class, ballroom

Wednesday
3am   Choir practice
4am   Long-jump training
5am   High-jump training
6am   Long-jump training again
7am   Trombone lesson
8am   Scuba-diving
9am to 4pm School

4pm Chef training
5pm Mountain climbing
6pm Tennis
7pm Drama workshop, Shakespeare and his contemporaries
8pm Show jumping

Thursday
2am Learning Arabic
3am Dance lesson, break-dance, hip-hop, krumping
4am Oboe lesson
5am Tour de France cycle training
6am Bible studies
7am Gymnastics training
8am Calligraphy class
9am to 4pm School
4pm Work experience shadowing a brain surgeon
5pm Opera singing lesson
6pm NASA space exploration workshop
7pm Cake baking class, level 5
8pm Attend lecture on 'A History of Victorian Moustaches'

Friday
1am Triangle lesson, grade 5
2am Badminton
3am Archery
4am Fly to Switzerland for ski-jump practice. Learn about eggs from an expert on eggs (TBC) on outbound flight.
6am Do quick ski-jump, and then board inbound flight. Take pottery class on flight.

8am   Thai kick-boxing (remember to take skis off before class).

9am to 4pm School

4pm   Channel swimming training

5pm   Motorbike maintenance workshop

6pm   Candle making

7pm   Otter rearing class

8pm   Television viewing. A choice between either a documentary about carpet manufacturing in Belgium, or a Polish cartoon from the 1920s about a depressed owl.

And that was just the weekdays. The weekends were when things *really* got busy for Annabelle. No wonder Chloe felt ignored.

'Well, I suppose things at home are . . . are . . .' stammered Chloe. She wanted to talk to him about it all, but she wasn't sure how.

Bong! Bong! Bong! Bong!

No, I haven't lost my mind, readers. That was meant to be the church clock striking four.

Chloe gasped and looked at her watch. Four o'clock! Mother made her do her homework from four until six every day, even in the school holidays when she didn't have any to do.

'Sorry Mr Stink, I have to go,' she said. Secretly Chloe was relieved. No one had ever asked her how she felt before, and she was beginning to panic . . .

21

'Really, child?' said the old man, looking disappointed.

'Yes, yes, I need to get home. Mother will be furious if I don't get at least a C in Maths next term. She sets me extra tests during the holidays.'

'That doesn't sound much like a holiday to me,' said Mr Stink.

Chloe shrugged. 'Mother doesn't believe in holidays.' She stood up. 'I hope you liked the sausages,' she said.

'They were scrumptious,' said Mr Stink. 'Thank you. Unimaginable kindness.'

Chloe nodded and turned to run off towards home. If she took a short-cut she'd be back before Mother.

'Farewell!' Mr Stink called after her softly.

4

DRIVEL

Terrified of being late for homework hour, Chloe began to quicken her pace. She didn't want her mother to ask questions about where she'd been or who she'd been talking to. Mrs Crumb would be horrified to find out her daughter had been sitting on a bench with someone she would describe as a 'soap-dodger'. Grown-ups always have a way of ruining everything.

Chloe stopped hurrying, though, when she saw that she was about to pass Raj's shop. *Just one chocolate bar*, she thought.

Chloe's love of chocolate made her one of Raj's best customers. Raj ran the local newsagent shop. He was a big jolly jelly of a man, as sweet and colourful as his slightly over-priced confectionery. Today, though, what Chloe really needed was some advice.

And maybe some chocolate. Just one bar, of course. Maybe two.

'Ah, Miss Chloe!' said Raj, as she entered the shop. 'What can I tempt you with today?'

'Hello, Raj,' said Chloe smiling. She always smiled when she saw Raj. It was partly because he was such a lovely man, and partly because he sold sweets.

'I have some Rolos on special offer!' announced Raj. 'They have gone out of date and hardened. You may lose a tooth as you chew into one, but at

10p off you can't really argue!'

'Mmm, let me think,' said Chloe scouring the racks and racks of confectionery. 'I had half a Lion bar earlier, you are welcome to make me an offer on the other half. I'll take anything upwards of 15p.'

'I think I'll just take a Crunchie, thanks Raj.'

'Buy seven Crunchie bars you get an eighth Crunchie bar absolutely free!'

'No thanks, Raj. I only want one.' She put the money down on the counter. 35p. Money well spent considering the nice feeling the chocolate would give her as it slipped down her throat and into her tummy.

'But Chloe, don't you understand? This is a unique opportunity to enjoy the popular chocolate-covered honeycomb bar at a dramatic saving!'

'I don't need eight Crunchie bars, Raj,' said Chloe. 'I need some advice.'

'I don't think I am really responsible enough to give out advice,' replied Raj without a hint of irony. 'But I'll try.'

Chloe loved talking to Raj. He wasn't a parent or a teacher, and whatever you said to him, he would never judge you. However, Chloe still gulped slightly, because she was about to attempt another little lie. 'Well, there's this girl I know at school . . .' she began.

'Yes? A girl at school. Not you?'

'No, somebody else.'

'Right,' said Raj.

Chloe gulped again and looked down, unable to meet his gaze. 'Well, this friend of mine, she's started to talk to this tramp, and she really likes talking to him, but her mother would blow a fuse if she knew, so I—I mean, my friend—doesn't know what to do.'

Raj looked at Chloe expectantly. 'Yes?' he said. 'And what is your question exactly?'

'Well Raj,' said Chloe. 'Do you think it's wrong to talk to tramps?'

'Well, it's not good to talk to strangers,' said Raj. 'And you should never let anyone give you a lift in a car!'

'Right,' said Chloe, disappointed.

'But a tramp is just somebody without a home,'

continued Raj. 'Too many people walk on by and pretend they're not there.'

'Yes!' said Chloe. 'That's what I think too.'

Raj smiled. 'Any of us could become homeless one day. I can see nothing wrong with talking to a tramp, just like you would anyone else.'

'Thanks Raj, I will . . . I mean, I'll tell her. This girl at school, I mean.'

'What's this girl's name?'

'Umm . . . Stephen! I mean Susan . . . no, Sarah. Her name is Sarah, definitely Sarah.'

'It's you, isn't it?' said Raj smiling.

'Yes,' admitted Chloe after a millisecond.

'You are a very sweet girl, Chloe. It's lovely that you would take the time to talk to a tramp. There but for the grace of God go you and I.'

'Thanks, Raj.' Chloe went a little red, embarrassed by his compliment.

'Now what can you buy your homeless friend for Christmas?' said Raj as he scoured around his disorganised shop. 'I have a box full of Teenage Mutant Ninja Turtles stationery sets I can't seem to shift. Yours for only £3.99. In fact buy one set, get ten free.'

'I'm not sure a tramp really has any need for a Teenage Mutant Ninja Turtles stationery set, thanks anyway Raj.'

'We all have use of a Teenage Mutant Ninja Turtles stationery set, Chloe. You have your Teenage Mutant Ninja Turtles pencil, your Teenage Mutant Ninja Turtles eraser, your Teenage Mutant Ninja Turtles ruler, your Teenage Mutant Ninja Turtles pencil case, your Teenage Mutant—'

'I get the idea, thanks, Raj, but I'm sorry, I'm not

26

going to buy one. I've got to go,' said Chloe, edging out of the shop as she unwrapped her Crunchie.

'I haven't finished, Chloe. Please, I haven't sold one! You also have your Teenage Mutant Ninja Turtles pencil sharpener, your Teenage Mutant Ninja Turtles notepad, your Teenage Mutant . . . oh, she's gone.'

*　　　*　　　*

'And what's this, young lady?' demanded Mother. She was standing waiting in Chloe's room. Between her thumb and index finger was one of Chloe's exercise books from school. Mother held it as if it were an exhibit in a court case.

'It's just my maths book, Mother,' said Chloe, gulping as she edged into the room.

You might think that Chloe was worried because her maths work wasn't up to scratch. But that wasn't quite it. The problem was, Chloe's maths book didn't have any maths in it! The book was supposed to be full of boring numbers and equations, but instead it was positively overflowing with colourful words and pictures. Spending so much time alone had turned Chloe's imagination into a deep dark forest. It was a magical place to escape to, and so much more thrilling than real life. Chloe had used the exercise book to write a story about a girl who is sent to a school (loosely based on her own) where all the teachers are secretly vampires. She thought it was much more exciting than boring equations, but Mother clearly didn't agree.

'If it is your mathematics book, why does it

27

contain this repulsive horror story?' said Mother.
This was one of those questions when you aren't
supposed to give an answer. 'No wonder you did so
poorly in your mathematics exam. I imagine you
have spent the time in class writing this . . . this
drivel. I am so disappointed in you, Chloe.'

Chloe felt her cheeks smarting with shame and
hung her head. She didn't think her story was
drivel. But she couldn't imagine telling her Mother
that.

'Don't you have anything to say for yourself?'
shouted Mother.

Chloe shook her head. For the second time in
one day she wanted to just disappear.

'Well, this is what I think of your story,' said
Mother, as she started trying to rip up the exercise
book.

'P-p-please . . . don't . . .' stammered Chloe.

'No, no, no! I'm not paying your school fees for you to waste your time on this rubbish! It's going in the bin!'

The book was obviously harder to rip than Mother had expected, and it took a few attempts to make the first tear. However, soon the book was nothing more than confetti. Chloe bowed her head, tears welling up in her eyes, as her mother dropped all the pieces in the bin.

'Do you want to end up like your father? Working in a car factory? If you concentrate on your maths and don't get distracted by silly stories, you have a chance of making a better life for yourself! Otherwise you'll end up wasting your life, like your father. Is that what you want?'

'Well, I—'

'How dare you interrupt me!' shouted Mother. Chloe hadn't realised this was another one of those questions you're not actually meant to answer. 'You'd better buck your ideas up, young lady!'

Chloe wasn't quite sure what that meant, but it didn't seem like the best time to ask. Mother left the room, dramatically slamming the door behind her. Chloe slowly sat down on the edge of her bed. As she buried her face in her hands, she thought of Mr Stink, sitting on his bench with only the Duchess for company. She wasn't homeless like him, but she *felt* homeless in her heart.

5

ABANDON STARBUCKS!

Monday morning. The first proper day of the Christmas holidays. A day Chloe had been dreading. She didn't have any friends she could text or email or SMS or Facebook or Twitter or whatever, but there was *one* person she wanted to see . . .

By the time Chloe got to the bench it was raining heavily, and she wished she'd at least paused to pick up an umbrella.

'The Duchess and I weren't expecting to see you again, Chloe,' said Mr Stink. His eyes twinkled at the surprise, despite the rain.

'I am sorry I ran off like that,' said Chloe,

'Don't worry, you are forgiven,' he chuckled.

Chloe sat down next to him. She gave the Duchess a stroke, and then noticed that the palm of her hand was black. She surreptitiously wiped it on her trousers. Then she shivered, as a raindrop ran down the back of her neck.

'Oh, no, you're cold!' said Mr Stink. 'Shall we take shelter from the rain in a coffee shop establishment?'

'Err . . . yes, good idea,' said Chloe, not sure if taking someone quite so stinky into an enclosed space really *was* a good idea. As they walked into the town centre, the rain felt icy, almost becoming hail.

When they arrived at the coffee shop, Chloe peered through the steamed-up glass window. 'I don't think there's anywhere to sit down,' she said. Unfortunately, the coffee shop was full to bursting with Christmas shoppers, trying to avoid the cruel British weather.

'We can but try,' said Mr Stink, picking up the Duchess and attempting to conceal her under his tweed jacket.

The tramp opened the door for Chloe and she squeezed herself inside. As Mr Stink entered, the pleasing aroma of freshly-brewed coffee keeled over and died. His own special smell replaced it. There was silence for a moment. Then panic.

People started running towards the door, clutching serviettes to their mouths as makeshift gas masks.

'Abandon Starbucks!' screamed a member of staff, and his colleagues immediately stopped making coffees or bagging muffins and ran for

31

their lives.

'It seems to be thinning out a little,' announced Mr Stink.

Soon they were the only ones left in the shop. *Maybe smelling this bad has its advantages*, thought Chloe. If Mr Stink's super-smell could empty a coffee shop, what else could it do? Maybe he could clear the local ice rink of skaters so she could have it all to herself? Or they could go to Alton Towers together and not have to queue for a single ride? Better still, she could take him and his smell into school one day, and if he was particularly stinky the headmistress would have to send everyone home and she could have the day off!

'You take a seat here, child,' said Mr Stink. 'Now, what would you like to drink?'

'Er . . . a cappuccino, please,' replied Chloe, trying to sound grown-up.

'I think I'll have one too.' Mr Stink shuffled behind the counter and started opening tins. 'Righty-ho, two cappuccinos coming right up.'

The machines hissed and spat for a few moments, and then Mr Stink pottered back over to the table with two mugs of a dark, unidentifiable liquid. On closer inspection, it appeared to be some kind of black slime, but Chloe was too well brought up to complain and pretended to sip whatever it was that he had concocted for her. She even managed an almost convincing, 'Mmm . . . lovely!'

Mr Stink stirred his solid liquid with a dainty little silver spoon he pulled out from his breast pocket. Chloe stole a glance at it and noticed it was monogrammed, with three little letters delicately engraved on the handle. She tried to get a better look, but he put it away before she could see what the letters were. What could they mean? Or was this simply another item Mr Stink had purloined during his career as a gentleman thief?

'So, Miss Chloe,' said Mr Stink, breaking her train of thought. 'It's the Christmas holidays, isn't it?' He took a sip from his coffee, holding his mug elegantly between his fingers. 'Why aren't you at home decorating the tree with your family or wrapping presents?'

'Well, I don't know how to explain . . .' No one in Chloe's family was good at expressing their feelings. To her mother, feelings were at best an embarrassment, at worst a sign of weakness.

'Just take your time, young lady.'

Chloe took a deep breath and it all came flooding out. What started off as a stream soon became a rushing river of emotion. She told him how her parents argued most of the time and how once she was sitting on the stairs when she heard her Mother shout, 'I am only staying with you for the sake of the girls!'

How her little sister made her life a misery. How nothing she did was ever good enough. How if she brought home some little bowl she had made in pottery class her Mother would put it at the back of a cupboard, never to be seen again. However, if her little sister brought any piece of artwork home, however awful, it was put in pride of place behind bulletproof glass as if it was the *Mona Lisa*.

Chloe told Mr Stink how her mother was always trying to force her to lose weight. Up until recently, Mother had described her as having 'puppy fat'. But once she turned twelve, Mother rather cruelly started calling it 'flab' or even worse

33

'blubber', as if she was some species of whale. Perhaps Mother was trying to shame her into losing weight. In truth, it only made Chloe more miserable, and being miserable only made her eat more. Filling herself up with chocolate, crisps and cake felt like being given a much-needed hug.

She told Mr Stink how she wished her dad would stand up to her mother sometimes. How she didn't find it easy to make friends, as she was so shy. How she only really liked making up stories, but it made her mother so angry. And how Rosamund ensured that every day at school was an absolute misery.

It was a long, long list, but Mr Stink listened intently to everything she said as jolly Christmas songs played incongruously in the background. For someone who spent every day with only a little black dog for company, he was surprisingly full of wisdom. In fact, he seemed to relish the opportunity to listen and talk and help. People didn't really stop to talk to Mr Stink—and he seemed pleased to be having a proper conversation for once.

He told Chloe, 'Tell your Mother how you feel, I am sure she loves you and would hate you to be unhappy.' And, '. . . try and find something fun you can do with your sister.' And, '. . . why not talk to your dad about how you feel?'

Finally, Chloe told Mr Stink about how Mother had ripped her vampire story to shreds. She had to try very hard not to cry.

'That's terrible, child,' said Mr Stink. 'You must have been devastated.'

'I hate her,' said Chloe. 'I hate my mother.'

'You shouldn't say that,' said Mr Stink.

'But I do.'

'You are very angry with her, of course, but she loves you, even if she finds it hard to show it.'

'Maybe.' Chloe shrugged, unconvinced. But having talked everything through she felt a little calmer now. 'Thank you so much for listening to me,' she said.

'I just hate to see a young girl like you looking sad,' said Mr Stink. 'I may be old, but I can remember what it was like to be young. I just hope I helped a little.'

'You helped a lot.'

Mr Stink smiled, before letting the last sludge of his volcanic gloop slip down his throat. 'Delicious! Now, we'd better leave some money for our beverages.' He searched around in his pockets for some change. 'Oh, bother, I can't read the board without my spectacles. I'll leave six pence. That should be enough. And a tuppence tip. They will be pleased with that. They can treat themselves to one of those new-fangled video cassettes. Right, I think you'd better be heading home now, young lady.'

The rain had stopped when they left the coffee shop. They sauntered down the road as cars hummed past.

'Let's swap places,' said Mr Stink.

'Why?'

'Because a lady should always walk on the inside of the pavement and a gentleman on the outside.'

'Really?' said Chloe. 'Why?'

35

'Well,' replied Mr Stink, 'the outside is more dangerous because that's where the cars are. But I believe it was originally because in the olden days people used to throw the contents of their chamber pots out of their windows and into the gutter. The person on the outside was more likely to get splattered!'

'What's a chamber pot?' said Chloe.

'Well I don't wish to be crude, but it's a kind of portable toilet.'

'Ugh! That's gross. Did people do that when you were a boy?'

Mr Stink chuckled. 'No, that was a little before my time, child. In the sixteenth century, in fact! Now, Miss Chloe, etiquette demands we swap places.'

His old-world gallantry was so charming it made Chloe smile, and they changed places. They strolled side by side, passing high-street shop after high-street shop, all trying to herald the approach of Christmas louder than the next. After a few moments Chloe saw Rosamund walking towards them with a small flotilla of shopping bags.

'Can we cross the road, please? Quickly,' whispered Chloe anxiously.

'Why, child? Whatever is the matter?'

'It's that girl from school I just told you about, Rosamund.'

'The one who stuck that sign to your back?'

'Yes, that's her.'

'You need to stand up to her,' pronounced Mr Stink. 'Let her be the one to cross the road!'

'No . . . please don't say anything,' pleaded Chloe.

'Who is this? Your new boyfriend?' laughed Rosamund. It wasn't a real laugh, like people do when they find something funny. That's a lovely sound. This was a cruel laugh. An ugly sound.

Chloe didn't say anything, just looked down.

'My daddy just gave me £500 to buy myself whatever I wanted for Christmas,' said Rosamund. 'I blew the lot at Topshop. Shame you're too fat to get into any of their clothes.'

Chloe merely sighed. She was used to being hounded by Rosamund.

'Why are you letting her talk to you like that, Chloe?' said Mr Stink.

'What's it to you, Grandad?' said Rosamund mockingly. 'Hanging around with smelly old tramps now, are you Chloe? You *are* tragic! How long did it take you to find that sign on your back

37

then?'

'She didn't find it,' said Mr Stink, slowly and deliberately. 'I did. And I didn't find it amusing.'

'Didn't you?' said Rosamund. 'All the other girls found it really funny!'

'Well, then they are as vile as you,' said Mr Stink.

'*What*?' said Rosamund. She wasn't used to being talked to like that.

'I said "then they are as vile as you",' he repeated, even louder this time. '*You* are a nasty little bully.' Chloe looked on anxiously. She hated confrontation.

To make matters worse, Rosamund took a pace forward and stood eye to eye with Mr Stink. 'Say that to my face, you old stinker!'

For a moment Mr Stink fell silent. Then he opened his mouth and let out the deepest darkest dirtiest burp.

'BBBBBBBBBBBBBBBBBBBBBBBBB
BBBBBBBBBBBBBBBBBBBBBBBBB
BBBBBBBBBBBBUUUUUUUU
UUUUUUUUUUUUUUUUUUU
UUUUUUUUUUUUUUUUUUU
URRRRRRRRRRRRRRRRRRR
RRRRRRRRRRRRRRRRRRRR
RRRRRRRRRRRRRRRRRRRR
RRRPPPPPPPPPPPPPPPPPPP
PPPPPPPPPPPPPPPPPPPPPP
PPPPPPPPPPPPPPPPPP!!!!!!!!!!!!!!
!!
! ! ! ! ! ! ! ! ! ! ! ! ! '

Rosamund's face turned green. It was as if a putrid tornado had engulfed her. It was the smell of coffee and sausages and rotten vegetables recovered from bins all rolled into one. Rosamund turned and ran, hurtling down the high street in such a panic that she dropped her TopShop bags on the way.

'That was so funny!' laughed Chloe.

'I didn't mean to belch. Most impolite. It was just that coffee repeating on me. Dear me! Now next time I want to see you stand up for yourself, Miss Chloe. A bully can only make you feel bad about yourself if you *let* them.'

'OK . . . I'll try,' said Chloe. 'So . . . see you tomorrow?'

'If you really want to,' he replied.

'I would love to.'

'And I would love to too!' he said, his eyes twinkling and twinkling as the last golden glow of the sunlight splintered through the sky.

At that moment a 4x4 thundered past. Its giant tyres sloshed through a huge puddle by the bus stop, sending up a wave that soaked Mr Stink from dirty head to dirty foot.

Water dripping from his glasses, he gave Chloe a little bow. 'And that,' he said, 'is why a gentleman always walks on the outside.'

'At least it wasn't a chamber pot!' chuckled Chloe.

6

SOAP-DODGERS

The next morning Chloe pulled open her curtains. Why was there a giant 'O' and a giant 'V' stuck to her window? She went outside in her dressing gown to investigate.

'VOTE CRUMB!' was spelled out in giant letters across the windows of the house. Elizabeth the cat pattered out with a rosette emblazoned with the words 'Crumb for MP' attached to her jewel-encrusted collar.

Then Annabelle came skipping out of the house with an air of self-congratulatory joy that was instantly annoying.

'Where are you going?' asked Chloe.

'As her favourite daughter, Mother has entrusted *me* with the responsibility of putting these leaflets through every door in the street. She's standing to be a Member of Parliament, remember?'

'Let me see that,' said Chloe, reaching out to grab one of the leaflets. The two warring sisters had long since dispensed with 'please' and 'thank you'.

Annabelle snatched it back. 'I am not wasting one on you!' she snarled.

'Let me see!' Chloe pulled the leaflet out of Annabelle's hand. There were some advantages to being the older sister; sometimes you could use brute force. Annabelle huffed off with the rest of the leaflets. Chloe walked back into the house studying it, her slippers moistening with the dew.

Mother was always going on and on about how she should run the country, but Chloe found the whole subject so dreary and dull that her imagination would float away into la-la land whenever the subject came up.

On the front of the leaflet was a photograph of Mother looking incredibly serious, with her finest pearls around her neck, her hair so waxy with spray that it would become a fireball if you put a lit match to it. Inside was a long list of her policies.

1) A curfew to be introduced to ensure all children under 30 are not allowed out after 8pm and are preferably in bed with lights out by 9pm.

2) The police to be given new powers to arrest people for talking too loudly in public.

3) Litterbugs to be deported.

4) The wearing of leggings to be outlawed in public areas, as they are 'extremely common'.

5) The national anthem to be played in the town square every hour on the hour. Everyone must be upstanding for this. Being in a wheelchair is no excuse for not paying your respects to Her Majesty.

6) All dogs to be kept on leads at all times. Even indoors.

7) Verruca socks to be worn by everyone attending the local swimming pool whether they have a verruca or not. This should cut down the chance of verruca infection to less than zero.

8) The Christmas pantomime to be discontinued due to the consistent lewdness of the humour (jokes about bottoms, for example. There is nothing funny about a bottom. We all have a bottom and we all know full well what comes out of a bottom and what sound a bottom can make of its own accord).

9) Church-going on Sunday morning to be compulsory. And when you do go you have to sing the hymns properly, not just open and close your mouth when the organ plays.

10) Mobile telephonic devices to have only classical music ringtones from now on, like Mozart and Beethoven and one of the other

ones, not the latest pop songs from the hit parade.

11) Unemployed people not to be allowed to claim benefit any more. Dole scum only have themselves to blame and are just plain idle. Why should we pay for them to sit at home all day watching or appearing on *The Jeremy Kyle Show*?

12) Giant bronze statues of royals Prince Edward and his fragrant wife Sophie, Countess of Wessex, to be erected in the local park.

13) Tattoos on anyone but visiting sailors to be banned. Tattoos can be dropped off anonymously at police stations without prosecution.

14) Fast food burger restaurants to introduce plates, cutlery and table service. And stop serving burgers. And French fries. And nuggets. And those apple pies that are always too hot in the middle.

15) The local library to stock only the works of Beatrix Potter. Apart from *The Tale of Mr Jeremy Fisher*, as the sequence when the frog, Mr Fisher, is swallowed by a trout is far too violent even for adults.

16) Football games in the local park are a nuisance. From now on only imaginary balls to be used.

17) Only nice films to be offered for rental in Blockbuster. That is to say films about posh people from the olden days who are too shy even to hold hands.

18) To combat the growing problem of 'hoodies' all hooded tops to have the hoods cut off.

19) Video games rot the brain. Any video games (or computer games or console games or whatever the stupid things are called) to be played only between 4pm and 4:01pm daily.

20) Finally, all homeless people, or 'soap-dodgers', are to be banned from our streets. They are a menace to society. And, more importantly, they smell.

Chloe slumped down on the sofa when she read these last sentences. There was a loud squeak as she did so. Mother had insisted on keeping on the plastic covers the sofa and armchair had arrived in, so as to keep them immaculate. They were indeed still immaculate, but it meant your bum got really hot and sweaty.

What about my new friend Mr Stink? Chloe thought. *What's going to happen to him? And what about the Duchess? If he is banned from the streets where on earth is he going to go?*

And then, a moment later, *Wow, my bum is getting incredibly hot and sweaty.*

She chaffed her way sadly back up the stairs to her room. Sitting on her bed, she stared out of the window. Because she was shy and awkward, Chloe didn't make friends easily. Now her newest friend Mr Stink was going to have to leave the town. Maybe for ever. She stared out through the glass at the deep blue endless air. Then, just before her eyes lost focus in the infinite sky of nothing, she looked down. The answer was at the end of the garden staring back at her.

The shed.

7

A BUCKET IN THE CORNER

This operation had to be top-secret. Chloe waited until darkness fell, and then led Mr Stink and the Duchess silently down her street, before slipping through the side gate to her garden.

'It's just a shed . . .' said Chloe apologetically as they entered his new abode. 'I'm sorry there's no ensuite bathroom, but there is a bucket in the corner there just behind the lawnmower. You can use that if you need to go in the night . . .'

'Well, this is unimaginably kind, young Miss Chloe, thank you,' said Mr Stink, smiling broadly. Even the Duchess seemed to bark 'thank you', or at least 'cheers'. 'Now,' continued Mr Stink, 'are you sure your mother and father don't mind me being here? I would hate to be an unwelcome guest.'

Chloe gulped, nervous about the lie that was about to come out of her mouth. 'No . . . no . . . they don't mind at all. They're just both very busy people and they apologise that they weren't able to be here right now to meet you in person.'

Chloe had carefully picked the right time to settle Mr Stink in. She knew Mother was out campaigning for election, and Dad was picking up Annabelle from her sumo-wrestling class.

'Well I would love to meet them both,' said Mr Stink, 'and see what people turned out such a wonderfully generous and thoughtful daughter. This will be so much warmer than my bench.'

Chloe smiled shyly at the compliment. 'Sorry there are all these old cardboard boxes in here,' she said. She started to move them out of the way, to give him room to lie down. Mr Stink gave her a hand, lifting some of the boxes on top of each other. When she got to the bottom box, Chloe paused. Poking out of the top was a charred electric guitar. She examined it for a moment, puzzled, then rummaged through the box and found a pile of old CDs. They were all the same, stacks and stacks of an album entitled *Hell For Leather* by The Serpents of Doom.

'Have you ever heard of this band?' she asked.

'I don't really know any music past 1958, I'm afraid.'

Chloe studied the picture on the cover for a moment. Super-imposed in front of a drawing of a giant snake stood four long-haired, leather-jacketed types. Chloe's eyes fixed on the guitar player, who looked an *awful* lot like her dad, only with a mess of curly black hair.

'I don't believe it!' said Chloe. 'That's my dad.'

She hadn't had any idea her dad had ever had a perm, let alone that he'd been in a rock band! She didn't know which was more shocking—the idea of him not being bald, or the idea of him playing electric guitar.

'Really?' said Mr Stink.

'I think so,' said Chloe. 'It looks like him anyway.' She was still studying the album cover with a curious combination of pride and embarrassment.

'Well, we all have secrets, Miss Chloe. Now what should I do if I require a pot of tea or a round of sausage sandwiches on white bread please with HP

47

sauce on the side? Is there a bell I should ring?'

Chloe looked at him, a little surprised. She hadn't realised she was going to have to feed him as well as shelter him.

'No, there's no bell,' she said. 'Erm, you see that window up there? That's my bedroom.'

'Ah yes?'

'Well if you need something, why don't you flash this old bicycle light up at my window? Then I can come down and . . . erm . . . take your order.'

'Perfection!' exclaimed Mr Stink.

Being in the confined space of the shed with Mr Stink was beginning to make it difficult for Chloe to breathe. The smell was especially bad today. It was stinky even by Mr Stink's stinky standards. 'Would you like to have a bath before my family get back?' Chloe said hopefully. The Duchess looked up at her master with a look of desperate hope in her blinking eyes. It was the stink that made her blink.

'Let me think . . .'

Chloe smiled at him expectantly.

'Actually, I'll leave it for this month, thank you.'

'Oh,' said Chloe, disappointed. 'Is there anything I can get you right now?'

'Is there an afternoon tea menu perhaps?' asked Mr Stink. 'A choice of scones, cakes and French pastries?'

'Erm . . . no,' said Chloe. 'But I could bring you a cup of tea and biscuits. And we should have some cat food that I could bring for the Duchess.'

'I am pretty sure the Duchess is a dog not a cat,' pronounced Mr Stink.

'I know, but we only have a cat, so we've only got cat food.'

'Well, maybe you could pop into Raj's shop tomorrow and buy the Duchess some tins of dog food. Raj knows the brand she likes.' Mr Stink rummaged in his pockets. 'Here's a ten pence piece. You can keep the change.'

Chloe looked in her hand. Mr Stink had actually placed an old brass button there.

'Thank you so much, young lady,' he continued. 'And please don't forget to knock when you return in case I am getting changed into my pyjamas.'

What have I done? thought Chloe, as she made

49

her way across the lawn back to the house. Her
head was buzzing with more imaginary life-stories
for her new friend, but none of them seemed quite
right. Was he an astronaut who had fallen to earth
and, in the shock, lost his memory? Or perhaps he
was a convict who had escaped from prison after
serving thirty years for a crime he didn't commit?
Or, even better, a modern-day pirate who had
been forced by his comrades to walk the plank into
shark-infested waters, but against all the odds had
swum to safety?

One thing she knew for sure was that he did
really whiff. Indeed she could still smell him as she
reached the back door. The plants and flowers in
the garden seemed to have wilted with the smell.
They were all now leaning away from the shed as if
they were trying to avert their stamens. *At least he's
safe*, thought Chloe. *And warm, and dry, if only for
tonight.*

When she got up to her room and looked out of
the window, the light was flashing already. 'All-
butter highland shortbread biscuits if you have
them, please!' called up Mr Stink. 'Thank you so
much!'

8

MAYBE IT'S THE DRAINS

'What's that smell?' demanded Mother as she entered the kitchen. She had been out all day campaigning and looked stiffly immaculate as ever in a royal blue twin-set—except for her nose, which was twitching uncontrollably in disgust.

'What smell?' said Chloe, with a short delay as she gulped.

'You must be able to smell it too, Chloe. That smell of . . . Well, I'm not going to say what it reminds me of, that would be impolite and unbecoming of a woman of my class and distinction, but it's a bad smell.' She breathed in and the smell seemed to take her by surprise all over again. 'My goodness, it's a very bad smell.'

Like a malevolent cloud of darkest brown, the smell had seeped through the timber of the shed, no doubt peeling off the creosote as it travelled. Then it had crept its way across the lawn, before opening the cat flap and starting its aggressive occupation of the kitchen. Have you ever wondered what a bad smell looks like? It looks like this . . .

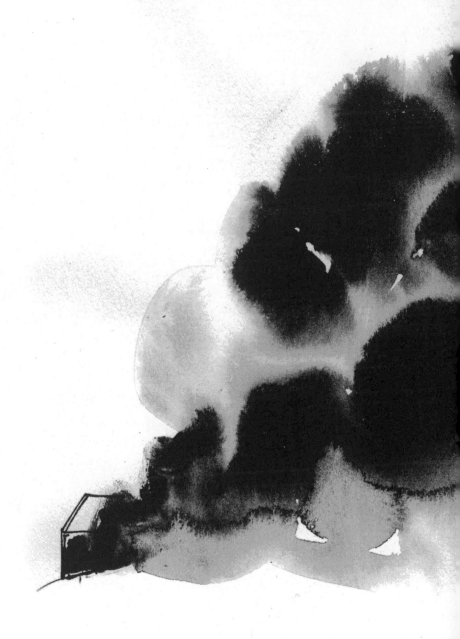

Oh, that's a nasty one. If you put your nose right
up against the page you can almost smell it.

'Maybe it's the drains?' offered Chloe.

'Yes, it must be the drains leaking again. Even

more reason why I need to be elected as an MP. Now, I have a journalist from *The Times* coming to interview me at breakfast tomorrow. So you must be on your best behaviour. I want him to see what a nice normal family we are.'

Normal?! thought Chloe.

'Voters like to see that one has a happy home life. I just pray that this foul stench will be gone by then.'

'Yes . . .' said Chloe. 'I'm sure it will. Mother, was Dad—I mean, Father—ever in a rock band?'

Mother stared at her. 'What on earth are you talking about, young lady? Where would you get such a ridiculous idea?'

Chloe swallowed. 'It's just I saw this picture of this band called The Serpents of Doom and one of them looked a lot like—'

Mother went a little pale. 'Preposterous!' she said. 'I don't know what's got into you!' She fiddled with her bouffant, almost as if she was nervous. 'Your father, in a rock band of all things! First that exercise book full of outrageous stories, and now this!'

'But—'

'No buts, young lady. Honestly, I don't know what to do with you any more.'

Mother looked really furious now. Chloe couldn't understand what she'd done wrong. 'Well, pardon me for asking,' she sulked.

'That's it!' shouted Mother. 'Go to bed, right now!'

'It's twenty past six!' Chloe protested.

'I don't care! Bed!'

Chloe found it hard to get to sleep. Not only because she had been sent to bed so ridiculously early, but also and more importantly because she had moved a tramp into the shed. She noticed the light of the torch bouncing off her bedroom window and looked at her alarm clock. It was

54

2:11am. What on earth could he want at this time of night?

Mr Stink had made the shed quite homely. He had fashioned a bed out of some piles of old newspapers. An old piece of tarpaulin was his duvet, with a grow bag for a pillow. It looked almost comfy. An old hosepipe had been arranged in the shape of a dog-basket for the Duchess. A plant-pot full of water sat beside for a bowl. In chalk he'd expertly drawn some old-fashioned portraits on the dark wooden creosoted walls, like the ones you see in museums or old country houses, depicting people from history. On one side he'd even drawn a window, complete with curtains and a sea view.

'You seem to be settling in then,' said Chloe.

'Oh, yes, I can't thank you enough, child. I love it. I feel like I finally have a home again.'

'I'm so pleased.'

'Now,' said Mr Stink. 'Miss Chloe, I called you down here because I can't sleep. I would like you to read me a story.'

'A story? What kind of story?'

'You choose, my dear. But I implore you, nothing too girly please . . .'

*   *   *

Chloe tiptoed up the stairs back to her room. Sometimes she liked to move around the house without making a sound, and so could remember where all the creaks were on the stairs. If she put her foot right in the middle of *this* step, or the left side of *this* one, she knew she wouldn't be heard. If she woke Annabelle up, she knew her little sister would relish the chance of getting her into deep deep trouble. And this wouldn't be normal everyday trouble like not eating your cabbage or 'forgetting' to do your homework. This would be 'inviting a tramp to live in the shed' trouble. It would be off the scale. As this simple graph shows:

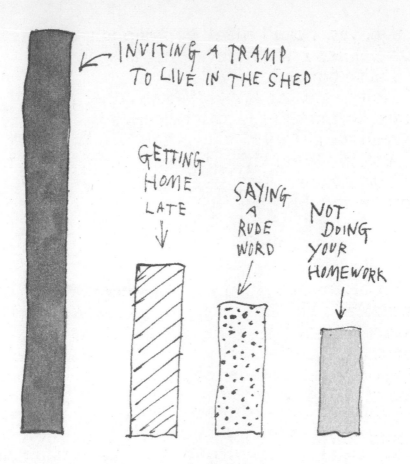

Alternatively, if you look at this simple Venn diagram you can see that if figure A is 'trouble' and figure B is 'serious trouble', then this shaded area here, representing inviting a tramp to live in the shed, is a sub-section of figure B:

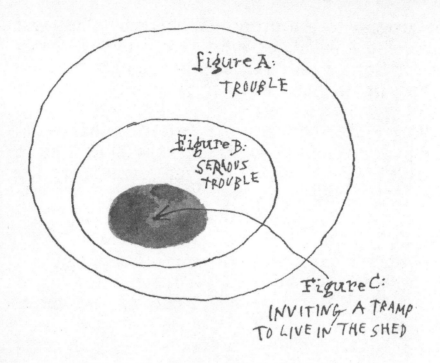

figure A:
TROUBLE

figure B:
SERIOUS
TROUBLE

figure C:
INVITING A TRAMP
TO LIVE IN THE SHED

I hope that makes things clear.

Chloe looked on her bookshelf, behind the little ornamental owls she collected even if she wasn't sure why. (Did she even *like* owls? Some distant aunt buys you a porcelain owl one day, some other aunt assumes you're collecting them, and by the end of your childhood you've got hundreds of the stupid things. Owls, not aunts.)

Chloe studied the spines of her books. They were quite girly. Lots of pinky-coloured books that matched her stupid pinky-coloured room that she hated. She hadn't chosen the colour of her walls. Hadn't even been asked. Why couldn't her room be painted black? Now *that* would be cool. Her mother only bought her books about ponies, princesses, ballet schools and brainless bleach-blonde teenagers in America whose only worry was what to wear to the prom. Chloe wasn't the least bit interested in any of them, and she was pretty sure Mr Stink wouldn't be either. The one story she had written had been torn to shreds by her mother. This wasn't going to be easy.

Chloe tiptoed back down the stairs and shut the kitchen door behind her incredibly slowly so it wouldn't make a noise, and then knocked gently on the shed door.

'Who is it?' came a suspicious voice.

'It's me, Chloe, of course.'

'I was fast asleep! What do you want?'

'You asked me to read you a story.'

'Oh well, now you've woken me up you better come in . . .'

Chloe took a last deep breath of the fresh night air and entered his den.

'Goody!' said Mr Stink. 'I used to love a bed-time story.'

'Well, actually I'm sorry, but I couldn't really find anything,' said Chloe. 'All my books are horribly girly. Most of them are pink, in fact.'

'Oh dear,' said Mr Stink. He looked disappointed for a moment, then he smiled at a thought. 'But what about one of your stories?'

'My stories?'

'Yes. You told me you like to make them up.'

'But I couldn't just . . . I mean . . . what if you don't like it?' Chloe's stomach fizzed with a peculiar mix of excitement and fear. No one had ever asked to hear one of her stories before.

'I'm sure I'll love it,' said Mr Stink. 'And anyhow, you'll never know until you try.'

'That's true,' said Chloe, nodding. She hesitated for a moment, then took a deep breath. 'Do you like vampires?' she asked.

'Well, I don't know any socially.'

'No, I mean, would you like to hear a story about vampires? These are vampires who are teachers in a school. Who suck the blood out of their poor unsuspecting pupils . . .'

'Is this the story your mother tore up?'

'Erm . . . yes,' replied Chloe sadly. 'But I think I can remember most of it.'

'Well, I would love to hear it!'

'Really?'

'Of course!'

'All right,' said Chloe. 'Please can you pass me the torch?'

Mr Stink passed it to her and she turned it on and put it under her face to look scary.

'Once upon a time . . .' she began, before losing her nerve.

'Yes?'

'Once upon a time . . . no, I can't do it! Sorry.'

Chloe hated reading out loud in class. She was so shy she would even try and hide under her desk to avoid it. This was even *more* terrifying. These were her words. It was much more private, more personal, and she suddenly felt like she wasn't ready to share it with anyone.

'Please, Miss Chloe,' said Mr Stink encouragingly. 'I really want to hear your story. It

60

sounds top banana! Now you were saying, once upon a time . . .'

She took a deep breath. 'Once upon a time, there was a little girl called Lily who hated going to school. It wasn't because the lessons were hard, it was because all her teachers were vampires . . .'

'Wonderful opening!'

Chloe smiled, and continued. Soon she was really getting into it, and putting on voices for her heroine Lily, Lily's best friend Justin who was bitten by the music teacher in a piano lesson and became a bloodsucker too, and Mrs Murk, the evil headmistress, who was in fact empress of vampires.

The tale unravelled all night. Chloe finished the story just before dawn as Lily finally drove her hockey stick through the headmistress's heart.

'. . . Mrs Murk's blood spurted out of her like newly struck oil, redecorating the sports hall a dark shade of crimson. The end.'

Chloe turned off the torch, her voice hoarse and her eyes barely still open.

'What an absolutely gripping yarn,' announced Mr Stink. 'I can't wait to find out what happens in book two.'

'Book *two*?'

'Yes,' said Mr Stink. 'Surely after killing the headmistress Lily is moved to another school. And all the teachers there could be flesh-eating zombies!'

That, thought Chloe, *is a very good idea*.

9

A LITTLE BIT OF DROOL

Chloe looked at her alarm-clock radio when she finally dropped into bed. 6:44am. She had never been to bed that late, ever. *Adults* didn't even go to bed that late. Maybe very naughty rock-star ones, but not many. She closed her eyes for a second.

'Chloe? *Chloeee*? Wake up! *Chloeeeeee*?' shouted Mother from outside the door. She knocked on the door three times. Then paused and knocked one more time which was especially annoying, as Chloe hadn't expected her to. She looked at the alarm-clock radio thing again. 6:45am. She had either been asleep for a whole day or a whole minute. As she couldn't open her eyes, Chloe guessed it must have been a minute.

'*Whaaaat . . .*?' she said, and was shocked by how deep and gravelly she sounded. Telling stories all night had turned Chloe's voice into that of a sixty-year-old ex-coal miner who smoked a hundred roll-ups a day.

'Don't "what" me, young lady! It's time you stopped lazing in bed. Your sister has already completed a triathlon this morning. Now get up. I need your help today on the campaign trail!'

Chloe was so tired she felt like she had grown into her bed. In fact, she wasn't sure where her body ended and the bed began. She slid out from under her duvet and crawled to the bathroom. Blinking in the mirror, Chloe thought for a moment that she was looking at her own nana. Then, sighing, she made her way downstairs and to the kitchen table.

'We are going campaigning today,' said Mother as she sipped her grapefruit juice and swallowed the motorway tailback of vitamin pills and food supplements she had lined up neatly on the table.

'It sounds *booorrrring*,' said Chloe. She made the word 'boring' sound even more boring by making it longer than it really needed to be. On Sunday mornings, Mother would allow the television to be switched on so she could watch programmes about politics. Chloe liked watching television. In a house where viewing was rationed, even an advert for a Stannah stair lift was a treat. However, these political discussion shows—which for no apparent reason were broadcast on Sunday mornings—were bum-numbingly boring. They made Chloe think that she wanted to be a kid forever if this was what the grown-up world was like.

Chloe always suspected that her mother had another motive for watching: she had a crush on the Prime Minister. Chloe couldn't see it herself, but lots of women her mother's age seemed to find him dishy. To Dad's amusement, Mother would always stop whatever she was doing to watch the PM if he came on the news. Once, Chloe had even spotted a little bit of drool ooze out of her mother's mouth when there was some footage of the Prime Minister in denim shorts playing Frisbee on a beach.

Of course, even the sight of her mother drooling didn't make those politics shows any less boring. But Chloe would have watched a hundred of them if it meant not having to spend the day campaigning with Mother. *That* was how boring it was going to be.

'Well, you are coming whether you like it or not,' said Mother. 'And put on that frilly yellow dress that I bought you for your birthday. You look almost pretty in that.'

Chloe did not look anywhere near pretty in it. She looked like a Quality Street. If that wasn't bad enough, she looked like one of the unpopular flavours that get left in the tin until way into the New Year. The only colour she really liked wearing was black. She thought black was cool, and even better it made her look less chubby. Chloe desperately wanted to be a Goth, but she didn't know where to start. You couldn't buy Goth clothes in Marks & Spencer's. And anyway, you also needed the white make-up and the black hair-dye, and most importantly the skill of looking down at your shoes at all times.

How would she go about becoming a Goth? Was there an application form to fill out? A committee of super-Goths who would vet you for Gothness, or was it Gothnicity? Chloe had once seen a real-life Goth hanging around by a bin in the high street and become incredibly excited. She really wanted to go over and ask her how to get started in the Goth world, but she was too shy. Which was ironic, since shyness is something you need if you want to be a successful Goth.

In the unlikely event of Elizabeth the cat becoming a Goth, she would look like this.

Fig A

Fig B

Let's get back to the story . . .

'It's cold outside, Chloe,' said Mother, when Chloe came downstairs in the horrible Quality Street dress. 'You'll need a coat. How about that tangerine-coloured coat your grandmother made you last Christmas?'

Chloe reached into the room under the stairs. This was where everyone in the family kept their coats and wellington boots. She heard a rustle in the darkness. Had Elizabeth the cat got shut in there by mistake? Or had Mr Stink moved indoors? She switched on the light. Peeking out from behind the bottom of an old fur coat was a frightened face.

'Dad?'

'Shush!'

'What are you hiding in here for?' Chloe whispered. 'You are meant to be at work.'

'No, I'm not. I lost my job at the factory,' said Dad sorrowfully.

'*What*?'

'A whole load of us got made redundant two weeks ago. No one is buying new cars right now.

It's the recession, I suppose.'

'Yes, but why are you hiding?'

'I'm too frightened to tell your mother. She'll divorce me if she finds out. Please, I beg you, don't tell her.'

'I'm not sure she'd div—'

'Please, Chloe. I'll sort all this out soon. It's not going to be easy, but I'll get another job if I can.'

He leaned forward so that the hem of the fur coat was draped over his head, the thick fur looking like a mess of curly hair.

'So that's what you look like with hair!' Chloe whispered.

'What?'

It was *definitely* Dad on that CD cover. With the fur over his head, he looked just like he did in the photo, with that astonishing perm!

'If you need a job, you could always go back to playing guitar with the Serpents of Doom,' said Chloe.

Dad looked startled. 'Who told you I was in a band?'

'I saw your CD and I asked Mother, but she—'

'Shh!' said Dad. 'Keep it down. Wait . . . where did you see this CD?'

'Er . . . I was . . . um . . . looking for my old hamster cage in the shed and it was in a box with a load of old junk. There was a burnt guitar with it.'

Dad opened his mouth to say something, but just at that moment, a door slammed upstairs.

'Come along, Chloe!' boomed Mother.

'Promise you won't say anything about me losing my job,' whispered Dad.

'I promise.'

Chloe shut the door, leaving her dad on all fours

in the darkness. Now she had two fully grown men hiding around the house. *What's next?* she thought. *Am I going to find Grandad in the tumble dryer?!*

10

SLIGHTLY CHEWED

Being on the political campaign trail meant Chloe knocking on what seemed like everybody's front door in the town and Mother asking people if she could 'rely on their vote'. Those who said they were going to vote for Mother were instantly rewarded with a big smile and an even bigger sticker to put in their window proclaiming 'Vote Crumb'. Those who said they *weren't* voting for her were going to miss an awful lot of daytime telly. Mother was the kind of person who wouldn't give up without a fight.

They passed the newsagent's shop. 'I wonder if Raj would put one of my posters up in his window,' said Mother, as she strode towards the store. Chloe clomped behind in her uncomfortable Sunday-best shoes, struggling to keep up. Her mind had been elsewhere all day. Now she was carrying around *two* hot-air balloon-sized secrets in her head—Mr Stink hiding in the garden shed and her dad hiding in the cupboard under the stairs!

'Ah, my two favourite customers!' exclaimed Raj as they entered the shop. 'The beautiful Mrs Crumb and her charming daughter, Chloe!'

'It's Crooooome!' corrected Mother. 'So, Raj, can I rely on your vote?'

'Are you on *The X-Factor*?!' said Raj excitedly. 'Yes, yes, of course I will vote for you. What are you singing on Saturday?'

'No, she's not doing *The X-Factor*, Raj,' interjected Chloe, trying not to laugh at the thought.

'*Britain's Got Talent* perhaps? You are maybe doing a ventriloquist act with a naughty otter puppet called Jeremy? That would be most amusing!'

'No, she's not doing *Britain's Got Talent* either.' Chloe smirked.

'*How do you solve any dream will I'd do anything* or whatever it's called with Graham thingy?'

'It's the election, Raj,' interrupted Mother. 'You know, the local election? I am standing to be our local MP.'

'And when is this election thing happening then?'

'Next Friday. I can't believe you've missed it! It's all over these newspapers, Raj!' Mother gestured at the piles and piles of newspapers in the shop.

'Oh, I only read *Nuts* and *Zoo*,' said Raj. 'I get all the news I need from them.'

Mother looked at him disapprovingly, even

though Chloe suspected she wasn't sure what either *Nuts* or *Zoo* were. Chloe had once seen a copy of *Nuts* that one of the older boys had brought into school, and knew it was rude.

'What do you think are the important issues facing Britain today, Raj?' asked Mother, delighted with the cleverocity and inteligentness of her own question.

Raj pondered for a moment, then shouted over at some boys who were loitering by the pick 'n' mix. 'Don't put the liquorice in your mouth unless you are going to buy it, young man! Oh dear, I will have to put that liquorice on special offer now!'

Raj grabbed a pen and a piece of card. He wrote 'slightly chewed', and put it on the liquorice box. 'Sorry, what was the question again?'

Note to self, thought Chloe. *Never buy liquorice from this shop again.*

'Erm . . . Now where was I?' said Mother to Raj. 'Ah yes, what do you think are the most—?'

'—important issues affecting Britain today, Raj?' chimed in Raj. 'Oh, I didn't need to say "Raj". I am Raj. Well, I think it would be a great advance if Cadbury's Creme Eggs were available not just at Easter but all year round. They are one of my most popular items. I also strongly believe that Quavers should diversify from cheese flavours to incorporate Asian Chicken and Lamb Rogan Josh varieties. And most importantly, and I know this may be controversial, but I think that coffee Revels should be banned as they spoil an otherwise wonderfully enjoyable confectionery. There, I've said it!'

'Right,' said Mother.

'And if you promise to change the government

policy on those issues you can rely on my vote, Mrs Crumb!'

Mother had had a mixed response to her campaigning so far, and was eager to secure this potentially crucial vote.

'Yes, I will certainly try, Raj!' she said.

'Thank you so much,' said Raj. 'Please help yourself to something from the shop.'

'No, I couldn't possibly, Raj!'

'Please, Mrs Crumb. Have a nice box of Terry's All Gold, I have only taken out the caramel squares. Mmm, they are delicious. And perhaps Chloe would like this Finger of Fudge? It's a bit squashed as my wife sat on it, but it's perfectly fine to eat.'

'We couldn't possibly accept these kind gifts, Raj,' said Mother.

'Well, why not buy them then? One box of Terry's All Gold, £4.29, and a Finger of Fudge, 20p. That's £4.49. Let's call it £4.50. Easier if I just take £5. Thank you so much.'

Chloe and Mother exited the shop holding their confectionery. Mother held her partially eaten box of chocolates with barely disguised disdain.

'Now, don't forget, Raj. The election is next Friday!' said Mother as she opened the door.

'Oh, I can't do next Friday, Mrs Crumb. I have to stay here as I am expecting a large shipment of Smarties! But good luck to you!'

'Ah . . . Thank you,' replied Mother, looking crestfallen.

'Mrs Crumb,' said Raj. 'May I interest you in something incredibly special that will certainly become something of a family heirloom to be passed down through the generations? Something

71

your grandchildren will one day take proudly to have valued on *The Antiques Road Show*?'

'Yes?' said Mother expectantly.

'It's a Teenage Mutant Ninja Turtles stationery set . . .'

11

HAIR PULLING

'What are you hiding in the shed?' said Annabelle with accusatory glee.

It was midnight and Chloe was once again tiptoeing past her sister's room, this time to tell Mr Stink about Lily's newest adventure with her flesh-eating zombie teachers. Annabelle stood in her doorway in her pink pony pyjamas. Her hair was in bunches. And in case of fire she slept in lip-gloss. She looked sickeningly cute.

'Nothing,' said Chloe, gulping.

'I know when you're lying, Chloe.'

'How?'

'You gulp when you tell a lie.'

'No I don't!' said Chloe, trying very hard not to gulp. She gulped.

'You just did! What's in there anyway? Have you got a boyfriend hiding in there or something?'

'No, I haven't got a boyfriend, Annabelle.'

'No, of course not. You would need to lose some weight first.'

'Just go back to bed,' said Chloe.

'I am not going to bed until you tell me what you've got in the shed,' announced Annabelle.

'Keep your voice down. You are going to wake everyone up!'

'No I won't keep my voice down! In fact it is going to get louder and louder. La la la la la la la la la la la la la la la la!'

'*Shush*!' hissed Chloe.

'La la la la la la la la la la la la la la la la la la la la la la la la la la la la la la la la la la la la la la la la la la la la la la la la la la la la la la la la la la la la la la la . . . !'

Chloe pulled her little sister's hair sharply. There was a pause for a moment, as Annabelle stared at Chloe in shock. Then she opened her mouth.

'AAAAAAAAAAAAAAAAAAAAAAA AAAAAAAAAAAAAAAAAAAAAAAAA AAAAAAAAAAAAAAAAAAAAAAAAA AAAAAAAAAAAAAAAAAAAAAAAAA

AAAAAAAAAAAAAAAAHHHHHHHH
HHHHHHHHHHHHHH!' wailed Annabelle.

'Girls! What on earth is all this noise?' said Mother as she sailed out of her bedroom in her silk nightgown.

Annabelle tried to speak, but hyperventilated through her tears.

'Ugh . . . eh . . . ah . . . eh . . . ah . . . ughhhh . . . ah . . . eh . . . ugh . . .'

'What on earth have you done to her, Chloe?' demanded Mother.

'She's putting it on! I didn't pull her stupid hair that hard!' Chloe protested.

'You pulled her *hair*? Annabelle is down to the last thousand for a model casting tomorrow for George at Asda and she has to look perfect!'

'Ugh . . . ah . . . eh . . . ah. She's ah eh got ugh ugh ugh hiding ugh ugh something eh ah ugh in the ugh ugh ughu shed,' said Annabelle as she squeezed out some more tears.

'Father,' ordered Mother. 'Come out here this instant!'

'I'm asleep!' came the muffled cry from their bedroom.

'THIS INSTANT!'

Chloe looked down at the carpet so Mother couldn't read her face. There was a pause. The three ladies of the house listened as Dad got out of bed. Next they heard the sound of someone passing water into a toilet bowl. Mother's face turned red with fury.

'I SAID THIS INSTANT!'

The sound abruptly stopped and Dad scurried out of the bedroom in his Arsenal FC pyjamas.

'Annabelle said Chloe is hiding something in the shed. Chocolate, most likely. I need you to go down there and take a look.'

'Me?' protested Dad.

'Yes you!'

'Can't it wait until the morning?'

'No it can't.'

'There's nothing down there,' pleaded Chloe.

'SILENCE!' demanded Mother.

'I'll just get a torch,' sighed Dad.

He made his way slowly downstairs, and Mother, Chloe and Annabelle rushed to the window of the master bedroom to watch him walk to the end of the garden. The moon was full, and it bathed the garden in an eerie glow. The torchlight danced around the trees and shrubs as he walked. They looked on breathlessly as Dad slowly opened the shed door. It creaked like a muffled scream.

Chloe could hear her heart beating. Was this the moment that would seal her doom forever? Would she be made to eat only cabbage for every meal from now on? Or get sent to bed before she'd even got up? Or be grounded for the rest of her life? Chloe gulped louder than she had ever gulped before. Mother heard this and shot her a look of dark, burning suspicion.

The silence was like thunder. A few seconds passed, or was it a few hours or even years? Then Dad emerged slowly from the shed. He looked up at the window and shouted, 'There's nothing here!'

12

PONGY PONG

Did I dream the whole thing? thought Chloe as she lay in bed. She was in that place between asleep and awake. That place where you can still remember dreaming. It was 4:48am, and now she was beginning to wonder if Mr Stink even really existed.

At dawn her curiosity got the better of her. Chloe edged down the stairs, and tiptoed across the cold wet grass to the shed door. She lingered outside for a moment, before opening it.

'Ah, there you are!' said Mr Stink. 'I am very hungry this morning. Poached eggs please, if it's not too much trouble. Runny in the middle. Sausages. Mushrooms. Grilled tomatoes. Sausages. Baked beans. Sausages. Bread and butter. Brown sauce on the side. Don't forget the sausages. English breakfast tea. And a glass of orange juice. Thank you so much.'

Chloe obviously hadn't dreamed the whole thing, but she was beginning to wish she had. It was all thrillingly, terrifyingly real.

'Freshly-squeezed orange juice to your liking, sir?' she asked sarcastically.

'Actually, have you got any that's very slightly off? I prefer that. Perhaps that was squeezed a month or so ago?'

Just then, Chloe spotted an old dog-eared black-and-white photograph that Mr Stink had placed on a shelf. It showed a beautiful young couple

77

standing proudly next to an immaculate and perfectly rounded Rolls-Royce, parked in the driveway of a magnificent stately home.

'Who's that?' she asked, pointing to the photo.

'Oh, nobody, n-n-n-nothing . . .' he stammered. 'Just a sentimental old photograph, Miss Chloe.'

'Can I see?'

'No, no, no, it's just a foolish picture. Please, pay it no heed.' Mr Stink was becoming increasingly flustered. He snatched the photograph from the shelf, and put it in his pyjama pocket. Chloe was disappointed. The photograph had seemed like another clue to Mr Stink's past, like his little silver spoon, or the way he'd bowled that piece of paper into the bin. This one had seemed like the best clue yet. But now Mr Stink was shoo-ing her out of the shed. 'Don't forget the sausages!' he said.

How on earth did Dad miss him? thought Chloe, as she went back to the house. Even if he hadn't seen Mr Stink in the shed, he surely must have smelled him.

Chloe tiptoed into the kitchen and opened the fridge door as quietly as possible. She stared into the fridge, and began carefully moving jars of mustard and pickle so they wouldn't clink. She hoped to find some out of date orange juice that might appeal to Mr Stink's tainted palate.

'What are you doing?' said a voice.

Chloe startled. It was only Dad, but she wasn't expecting to see him up this early. She gathered herself for a moment.

'Nothing, Dad. I'm just hungry that's all.'

'I know who's in the shed, Chloe,' he said.

Chloe looked at him, panicked, unable to think, let alone speak.

'I opened the shed door last night to see an old tramp snoring next to my lawnmower,' Dad went on. 'The pong was . . . well . . . pongy. It was an extremely pongy pong . . .'

'I wanted to tell you, honestly I did,' said Chloe. 'He needs a home, Dad. Mother wants all homeless people driven off the streets!'

'I know, I know, but I'm sorry Chloe, he can't stay. Your mother will go nuts if she finds out.'

'Dad, I'm sorry.'

'It's OK, love. I am not going to say anything to your mother. You've kept your promise not to tell anyone about me losing my job, haven't you?'

'Yes, of course.'

'Good girl,' said Dad.

'So,' said Chloe, glad to have Dad to herself for a while. 'How did your guitar get all burned?'

'Your mother put it on the bonfire.'

'No!'

'Yes,' said Dad sorrowfully. 'She wanted me to move on with my life. She was doing me a favour, I suppose.'

'A *favour*?'

'Well, The Serpents of Doom were never going to make it. I got the job at the car factory and that was that.'

'But you had an album! You must have been dead famous,' chirped Chloe excitedly.

'No, we weren't at all!' chuckled Dad. 'The album only sold twelve copies.'

'*Twelve*?' said Chloe.

'Yes, and your grandma bought most of those.

We were pretty good, though. And one of our singles got into the charts.'

'What, the top forty?'

'No, we peaked at 98.'

'Wow,' said Chloe. 'Top 100! That's pretty good, isn't it?'

'No, it isn't,' said Dad. 'But you're very sweet to say so.' He kissed her on the forehead and opened his arms to give her a hug.

'There's no time for cuddles!' said Mother as she strode into the kitchen. 'The man from *The Times* will be here soon. Father, you make the scrambled eggs. Chloe, you can lay the table.'

'Yes, of course, Mother,' said Chloe, with at least half her brain worrying about when Mr Stink was going to get his breakfast.

*   *   *

'So how important is your family to you, Mrs Crumb?' asked the serious-looking journalist. He wore thick glasses and was old. In fact he had probably been born an old man. Plopped out of his mother, wearing glasses and a three-piece suit. He was called Mr Stern, which Chloe thought was pretty fitting. He didn't look like he smiled a lot. Or indeed ever.

'Actually, it's pronounced Croombe,' corrected Mother.

'No, it's not,' said Dad before his wife shot him a look of utter fury. The Crumb family was sitting around the dining table and not enjoying their posh breakfast. It was all such a lie. They didn't normally sit round the dining room table eating smoked salmon and scrambled eggs. They would be round the *kitchen* table eating Rice Krispies or Marmite on toast.

'Very important, Mr Stern,' said Mother. 'The most important thing in my life. I don't know what I'd do without my husband, Mr Crooome, my darling daughter, Annabelle and the other one . . . whatshername? Chloe.'

'Well, then I ask you this Mrs . . . Crooooooome. Is your family more important to you than the future of this country?'

That was a toughie. There was a pause during which a civilization could rise and fall.

'Well, Mr. Stern . . .' Mother said.

82

'Yes, Mrs Croooooooooome . . . ?'

'Well, Mr Stern . . .'

'Yes, Mrs Crooooooooooooooooooooooooooo ooome . . . ?'

At that moment there was a little rat-tat-tat on the window. 'Excuse me for interrupting,' said Mr Stink with a smile, 'but please could I have my breakfast now?'

13

SHUT YOUR FACE!

'Who on earth is *he*?' enquired Mr Stern as Mr Stink trudged around in his filthy striped pyjamas to the backdoor.

There was silence for a moment. Mother's eyes bulged out of their sockets and Annabelle looked like she was about to shriek or vomit or both.

'Oh, he's the tramp who lives in our shed,' said Chloe.

'The tramp who lives in our shed?' repeated Mother incredulously. She looked at her husband with black fire in her eyes.

He gulped.

'I told you she was hiding something in there, Mother!' exclaimed Annabelle.

'He wasn't there when I looked!' protested Dad. 'He must have concealed himself behind a trowel!'

'What a wonderful woman you are, Mrs Crooooooooooome,' said Mr Stern. 'I read about your policies on the homeless. About driving them off the streets. I had no idea you meant we should drive them into our homes and let them come and *live* with us.'

'Well I . . .' spluttered Mother, lost for words.

'I can assure you I am going to write an absolutely glowing piece about you now. This will make the front page. You could be the next Prime Minister of the country!'

'My sausages?' said Mr Stink, as he entered the dining room.

'Excuse me?' said Mother, before putting her hand over her mouth in horror at the smell.

'Forgive me,' said Mr Stink. 'It's just that I asked your daughter Chloe for some sausages two hours ago, and my sincerest apologies, but I am getting rather peckish!'

'You say I could be the next Prime Minister of the country, Mr Stern?' said Mother, thoughtfully.

'Yes. It's so kind of you. Allowing a dirty old smelly tramp like this—I mean, no offence—'

'None taken,' replied Mr Stink without hesitation.

'—to come and live with you. How you could you *not* be elected as an MP now?'

Mother smiled. 'In that case,' she said, turning to Mr Stink, 'how many sausages would you like my very good friend who lives in my shed and hardly stinks at all?'

'No more than nine, please,' replied Mr Stink.

'Nine sausages coming right up!'

'With poached eggs, bacon, mushrooms, grilled tomatoes, bread and butter and brown sauce on the side, please.'

'Certainly, my extremely close and beloved friend!' came the voice from the kitchen.

'You smell so rank I think I'm going to die,' said Annabelle.

'That's not nice, Annabelle,' said Mother breezily from the kitchen. 'Now come and help me in here, darling, there's a good girl!'

Annabelle ran to the sanctuary of the kitchen. 'It stinks in here now as well!' she screamed.

'Shut your face!' snapped Mother.

'So, tell me . . . tramp,' said Mr Stern, leaning in towards Mr Stink before the smell got to him and he leaned back. 'Is it just you living in the shed?'

'Yes, just me. And of course my dog, the Duchess . . .'

'HE'S GOT A DOG?' cried Mother anxiously from next door.

'And how do you find living here?' continued Mr Stern.

'Nice,' said Mr Stink. 'But I warn you, the service is painfully slow . . .'

14

LADY AND THE TRAMP

'LADY AND THE TRAMP' was the headline.

Mr Stern had been true to his word and the story had made the front page of *The Times*. A large photograph of Mother and Mr Stink accompanied the piece. Mr Stink was smiling broadly, showing his blackened teeth. Mother was trying to smile, but because of the smell she had to keep her mouth firmly closed. As soon as the paperboy put the paper through the letterbox, the Crumbs pounced upon it and devoured it in a frenzy. Mother was famous! She read the article out loud with pride.

Mrs Crumb may not look like a political revolutionary in her smart blue suits and pearls, but she could well change the way we live our lives. She is standing for MP in her local town and, although her policies read as very hard line, she has taken the extraordinary step of inviting a tramp to live with her family.

'It was all my idea,' said Mrs Crumb (pronounced 'Crooooooooooooooome'). 'At first my family was dead against it, but I just had to give this poor filthy flea-ridden dirt-encrusted stomach-turningly smelly beggar-man and his abhorrent hound a home. I love them both dearly. They're part of the family now. I couldn't imagine life without them. If only other people were as beautifully kind-hearted as me.

A modern day saint, some people are saying. If every family in this country was to let a tramp live with them it could solve the problem of homelessness forever. Oh, and don't forget to vote for me in the forthcoming election.'

It's a genius idea, and could put Mrs Crumb in line to be the next Prime Minister.

The tramp, known only as 'Mr Stink' had this to say. 'Please could I trouble you for another sausage?'

'It wasn't your idea, Mother,' snapped Chloe, too angry to merely sulk.

'Not strictly speaking, dearest, no . . .'

Chloe glared at her, but at that moment the telephone tinkled.

'Get that will you, someone? It's probably for me,' said Mother, grandly.

Annabelle dutifully picked up the phone. 'Crooombe residence. Who is speaking please?' she asked, just as her mother had instructed her to. Mother even had a special telephone voice, a note posher than her usual one.

'Who is it, dear?' said Mother.

'It's the Prime Minister,' replied Annabelle, putting her hand over the mouthpiece.

'The *Prime Minister*?' squealed Mother.

She hurled herself towards the telephone.

'Mrs Croooombe speaking!' said Mother in a truly ridiculous voice, a good note posher than even her usual telephone one. 'Yes, thank you, Prime Minister. It was a super piece in the newspaper, Prime Minister.'

Mother was drooling again. Dad rolled his eyes.

'I would be delighted to be a guest on *Question*

Time tonight, Prime Minister,' said Mother.

Then she went quiet. Chloe could hear a murmur from the other end of the line, followed by silence.

Mother's jaw dropped open.

'*What?*' she growled into the phone, losing her poise and dignity for an instant.

Chloe looked at Dad questioningly and he shrugged.

'What do you mean, you want the tramp to go on as well?' said Mother, incredulous.

Dad grinned. *Question Time* was a serious political discussion programme hosted by a Sir. It was Mother's big chance to shine, and she obviously didn't want it ruined by a malodorous old tramp.

'Well, yes,' went on Mother, 'I know it makes a good story, but does he really have to be on too? He reeks!'

There was another pause while the Prime Minister spoke, the murmur getting a little bit louder. Chloe was impressed with the man. Anyone who could get Mother to stop talking for a moment *deserved* to run the country.

'Yes, yes, well, if that's what you really want Prime Minister, then yes, of course I will bring Mr Stink along. Thank you so much for calling. By the way I make a very moist Lemon Drizzle Cake. If you are ever passing by on your battle bus I would be delighted to offer you a slice or two. No? Well, goodbye . . . Goodbye . . . Goodbye . . .' She checked one last time that he had definitely gone. 'Goodbye.'

Chloe rushed into the garden to tell Mr Stink the news. She heard a 'Grrrrrr' and assumed it must be the Duchess. However, it was actually Elizabeth the cat who was growling. She was looking up at the roof of the shed, where a trembling Duchess was hiding. The little black dog was yelping softly. Chloe chased Elizabeth away, and eventually coaxed the Duchess down. She patted her.

'There, there,' she said. 'That nasty puss has gone now.'

Elizabeth flew out of the bushes and through the air like a kung-fu kitten. A terrified Duchess rocketed up the apple tree to safety. Elizabeth prowled around the trunk, hissing malevolently.

Chloe knocked on the shed door. 'Hello?'

'Is that you, Duchess?' came Mr Stink's voice from inside.

'No, it's Chloe,' said Chloe. *He's nuts!* she thought.

'Oh, lovely Chloe! Do come in, dear heart.'

Mr Stink upturned a bucket. 'Please, please take a seat. So did your mother and I make the newspaper?'

'You're on the front page. Look!'

She held up the paper and he let out a little chuckle. 'Fame at last!'

'And that's not all. We just had a call from the Prime Minister.'

'Winston Churchill?'

'No, we've got a new one now, and he wants you and mother to go on this programme called *Question Time* tonight.'

'On the televisual box?'

'The TV? Yes. And I was thinking, before you go on . . .' Chloe looked at Mr Stink hopefully. 'It might be a good idea if you had a . . .'

'Yes, child?'

'Well a . . .'

'Yes . . . ?'

'A . . .' She finally plucked up the courage to say it, '. . . bath?'

Mr Stink looked at her suspiciously for a few seconds.

'Chloe?' he asked at last.

'Yes, Mr Stink?'

'I don't smell, do I?'

How could she answer that? She didn't want to hurt Mr Stink's feelings, but then again it would be much easier to be around him if he were introduced to Mr Soap and his charming wife, Mrs Water . . .

'No, no, no, of course you don't smell,' said Chloe, gulping the biggest gulp that had ever been gulped.

'Thank you, my dear,' said Mr Stink, seeming almost convinced. 'Then why do people call me Mr Stink?'

In her head, Chloe heard the intensely dramatic

music from *Who Wants to be a Millionaire?* This could in fact have been the million pound question. But Chloe had no '50/50', no 'ask the audience' and not even a 'phone a friend' at her disposal. After a long pause, in which you could have watched all three *Lord of the Rings* films in their specially extended director's cuts, words started to form in Chloe's mouth.

'It's a joke,' she heard herself saying.

'A joke?' asked Mr Stink.

'Yes, because you actually smell really nice so everyone calls you Mr Stink as a joke.'

'Really?' His suspicion seemed to be thawing a little.

'Yes, like calling a really small man "Mr Big" or a very thin person "Fatso".'

'Oh, yes, I understand, most amusing!' chuckled Mr Stink.

The Duchess looked at Chloe with a look that said, *You had the chance to tell him, but you chose to carry on the lie.*

How do I know that the Duchess's look said this? Because there is an excellent book in my local library entitled *One Thousand Doggy Expressions Explained* by Professor L. Stone.

I digress.

'But,' said Chloe, 'you might like to have a bath, well, just for fun . . .'

15

BATH TIME

This was no ordinary bath time. Chloe realised this had to be run like a military operation.

Hot water? Check.

Towels? Check.

Bubble bath? Check.

Rubber duck or similar animal-based bath toy? Check.

Soap? Was there enough soap in the house? Or in the town? Or indeed in the whole of Europe, to make Mr Stink clean? He hadn't had a bath since—well, he claimed last year, but it might as well have been since dinosaurs ruled the earth.

Chloe turned on the taps, running them both together so the temperature would be just right. If it was too hot or too cold it might scare Mr Stink off baths for ever. She poured in some bubble bath, and gave it a swirl. Then she laid out some neatly folded towels, pleasingly warm from the airing cupboard, on a little stool by the bath. In the cabinet she found a multi-pack of soaps. It was all going perfectly according to plan, until . . .

'He's escaped!' said Dad, poking his head around the bathroom door.

'What do you mean, "escaped"?' said Chloe.

'He's not in the shed, he's not in the house, I couldn't see him in the garden. I don't know where he is.'

'Start the car!' said Chloe.

They sped off out of their street. This was

exciting. Dad was driving faster than usual, although still one mile an hour less than the speed limit, and Chloe sat in the front seat, which she hardly ever did. All they needed were some doughnuts and coffee to go, and they could be two mismatched cops in a Hollywood action movie. Chloe had a hunch that if Mr Stink was anywhere he would be back sat on his bench where she had first talked to him.

'Stop the car!' she said, as they passed the bench.

'But it's a double yellow line,' pleaded Dad.

'I said, stop the car!'

Dad stamped on the brake. The tyres screeched as the car stopped. They were both propelled forward a little in their seats. They smiled at each other at the excitement of it all—it was as if they had just ridden a rollercoaster. Chloe sprang out of the car and slammed the door shut, something she would never dare do if her mother were around.

But the bench was empty. Mr Stink wasn't there. Chloe sniffed the air. There was a faint whiff of him, but she couldn't really tell if this was a recent one or a lingering odour from a week or so ago.

Dad drove around the town for another hour. Chloe checked all the places she thought her tramp friend might be—under bridges, in the park, in the coffee shop, even behind bins. But it seemed as though he really had disappeared. Chloe felt like crying. Maybe he had left the town—he was a wanderer, after all.

'We'd better head home now, darling,' said Dad softly.

'Yep,' said Chloe, trying to be brave.

'I'll put the kettle on,' said Dad as they walked

indoors.

In Britain, a cup of tea is the answer to every problem.

Fallen off your bicycle? Nice cup of tea.

Your house has been destroyed by a meteorite? Nice cup of tea and a biscuit.

Your entire family has been eaten by a Tyrannosaurus Rex that has travelled through a space/time portal? Nice cup of tea and a piece of cake. Possibly a savoury option would be welcome here too, for example a Scotch egg or a sausage roll.

Chloe picked up the kettle and went to the sink to fill it. She looked out of the window.

Just then, Mr Stink's head popped up from the pond. He gave her a little wave. Chloe screamed.

When they'd got over their shock, Chloe and Dad walked slowly towards the pond. Mr Stink was humming the song 'Row row row your boat' to himself. As he sang, he rubbed algae into himself with a water lily. A number of goldfish floated upside down on the water's surface.

'Good afternoon, Miss Chloe, good afternoon, Mr Crumb,' said Mr Stink brightly. 'I won't be too long. I don't want to get too wrinkled in here!'

'What . . . what . . . what are you doing?' asked Dad.

'The Duchess and I are having a bath of course, as young Chloe suggested.'

At that moment the Duchess appeared out of the murky depths, covered in weeds. As if it wasn't enough that he was having a bath in a pond, Mr Stink had to share it with his dog too. After a few moments the Duchess clambered out of the pond, leaving behind a large black scum layer floating on the water. She shook herself dry and Chloe stared at her in surprise. It turned out she wasn't a little black dog after all, but a little white one.

'Mr Crumb, sir?' said Mr Stink. 'Would you mind awfully passing me a towel? Thank you so much. Ah! I am as clean as a whistle now!'

16

RULE BRITANNIA

Mother sniffed. And sniffed again. Her nose wrinkled with disgust.

'Are you sure you had a bath, Mr Stink?' she enquired, as Dad drove all the family and Mr Stink to the television studio.

'Yes, I did, Madam.'

'Well, there is a funny smell of pond in this car. And dog,' pronounced Mother from the front seat.

'I think I'm going to puke,' pronounced Annabelle from the back seat.

'I've told you before, darling. We don't say "puke" in this family,' corrected Mother. 'We say we are feeling very slightly nauseous.'

Chloe opened the window discreetly, so as not to hurt Mr Stink's feelings.

'Do you mind if we keep the window closed?' asked Mr Stink. 'I am a little chilly.'

The window went up again.

'Thank you so much,' said Mr Stink. 'Such unimaginable kindness.'

They stopped at some traffic lights and Dad reached for one of his hard rock CDs. Mother slapped his hand, and he put it back on the steering wheel. She then put her favourite CD on the car stereo, and the old couple in the next car looked at the Crumb family strangely as 'Rule Britannia, Britannia rules the waves' came blaring out of their car.

*   *   *

'Mmm, no no no, that won't do at all . . .' said the TV producer as he studied Mr Stink. 'Can we put some dirt on him? He doesn't look trampy enough. Make-up? Where's make-up?'

A lady with far too much make-up on appeared from around a corridor, scoffing a croissant and holding a powder-puff.

'Darling, have you got any grime?' asked the producer.

'Come this way, Mr . . . ?' said the make-up lady.

'Stink,' said Mr Stink proudly. 'Mr Stink. And I am going to star on the television tonight.'

Mother scowled.

Chloe, Annabelle and Dad were led to a little room with a television, half a bottle of warm white wine and some stale crisps, to watch the show

being broadcast live.

The thunderous title music started, there was polite applause from the audience and the pompous-looking presenter, Sir David Squirt addressed the camera. 'Tonight on *Question Time* it's an election special. We have representatives from all the major political parties, and also a tramp who goes by the name of Mr Stink. Welcome to the programme, everyone.'

Everyone around the table nodded, apart from Mr Stink who proclaimed loudly, 'May I say what a delight it is for me to be on your show tonight?'

'Thank you,' said the presenter uncertainly.

'Being homeless I have never seen it,' said Mr Stink. 'In fact, I have absolutely no idea who you are. But I am sure you are wildly famous. Please continue, Sir Donald.'

The audience laughed uncertainly. Mother

looked displeased. The presenter coughed nervously and tried to continue.

'So the first question tonight . . .'

'Are you wearing make-up, Sir Declan?' enquired Mr Stink innocently.

'A little, yes. For the lights of course.'

'Of course,' agreed Mr Stink. 'Foundation?'

'Yes.'

'Eye liner?'

'A little.'

'Lip-gloss?'

'A smidge.'

'Looks nice. I wish I'd had some now. Blusher?'

The audience chuckled throughout this exchange. Sir David moved on rapidly. 'I should explain that Mr Stink is here tonight as he has been invited to live with Mrs Crumb . . .'

'Crooommmbe,' corrected Mother.

'Oh,' said Sir David. 'I do apologise. We checked the pronunciation with your husband, and he said it was Crumb.'

Mother went red with embarrassment. Sir David turned his attention back to his notes. 'Later on in the programme,' he said, 'we will be discussing the difficult topic of homelessness.'

Mr Stink put his hand up.

'Yes, Mr Stink?' asked the presenter.

'May I just pop to the lavatory, Sir Duncan?'

The audience laughed louder this time.

'I should have gone before we started, but I asked the make-up lady to do my hair and it took forever. Don't get me wrong, I am thrilled with the results; she gave me a wash and blow-dry. They even put something called gel in it, but I didn't get a chance to go to the little boy's room.'

'Of course, if you need to go, go . . .'

'Thank you so, so much,' said Mr Stink. He rose to his feet and started to potter off the set. 'I shouldn't be too long, I think it's just a number one.'

The audience howled again with laughter. In the little room with the stale crisps and the television Chloe and Dad were laughing too. Chloe looked at Annabelle. She was trying not to laugh, but a smile was definitely creeping up her face.

'My apologies!' exclaimed Mr Stink as he crossed the stage again in the opposite direction. 'I am told the lavatory is this way . . .!'

17

COLLAPSED BOUFFANT

'And that's why I feel that there should be a curfew on all people under thirty.' Mother was in full flow now, and she smiled as she received a smattering of applause for this comment from the people over thirty in the audience. 'They should all be in bed by eight o'clock at the latest . . .'

'Sorry I was a while,' said Mr Stink as he ambled back on to the set. 'I thought it was just a number one, but while I was standing there I suddenly got the urge to have a number two.' The audience erupted into laughter, some even applauding in delight as this serious show descended into a discussion of an old tramp's toilet habits. 'I mean, I usually do my number twos in the mornings, between 9:07 and 9:08, but I had an egg sandwich backstage before I came on the show tonight. I don't know if you made the sandwiches, Sir Derek?'

'No, I don't make the sandwiches, Mr Stink. Now please can we get back to the question of curfews for young—'

'Well, it was a delicious sandwich, don't get me wrong,' said Mr Stink. 'But egg can sometimes make me want to go. And I don't always get that much of a warning, especially at my age. Do you ever have that problem, Sir Doris? Or do you have the bum of a much younger man?'

Another massive wave of laughter crashed on to the stage. In the stale crisps room even Annabelle was laughing now.

'We are here to discuss the serious topics of the day, Mr Stink,' continued Sir David. His face was redder than red with anger as his serious political programme, a programme he had presented for forty tedious years, was rapidly turning into a comedy show starring an old tramp. The audience was enjoying it immensely though, and booed Sir David a little as he tried to steer the show back to politics. He shot them a steely stare before turning to the new star of the show. 'And my name is Sir David. Not Sir Derek, or Sir Doris. *Sir David*. Now, let's move on to the question of homelessness, Mr Stink. I have a statistic here which says that there are over 100,000 homeless people in the UK today. Why do you think so many people are living on the streets?'

Mr Stink cleared his throat a little. 'Well, if I may be so bold, I would venture that part of the problem stems from the fact that we are seen as statistics rather than people.' The audience applauded and Sir David leaned forward with interest. Perhaps Mr Stink wasn't the clown he had taken him for.

'We all have different reasons for being homeless,' continued Mr Stink. 'Each homeless person has a different story to tell. Perhaps if people in the audience tonight, or out there watching at home, stopped to *talk* to the homeless people in their town, they would realise that.'

The audience were applauding even louder now, but Mrs Crumb leaped in. 'That's what I did!' she exclaimed. 'I just stopped to talk to this tramp one day and then asked him to come and live with my family. I've always put others before myself. I suppose that's always been my downfall,' she said, tilting her head to the side and smiling at the audience as if she were an angel sent down from heaven.

'Well, that's not really true is it, Mrs Crumb?' said Mr Stink.

There was silence. Mother stared at Mr Stink in horror. The audience shifted excitedly in their seats. Dad, Annabelle and Chloe all leaned forward closer to the television. Even Sir David's moustache twitched in anticipation.

'I don't know what you mean, my very close friend . . .' squirmed Mrs Crumb.

'I think you do,' said Mr Stink. 'The fact is, it wasn't *you* who invited me in, was it?'

Sir David's eyes gleamed. 'Then who *did* invite you to stay with the Crumb family, Mr Stink?' he enquired, back in his stride now.

'Mrs Crumb's daughter, Chloe. She's only twelve but she's an absolutely fantastic girl. One of the sweetest, kindest people I have ever met.'

These words fell on Chloe like an enormous YES. Then everyone in the stale crisps room looked towards her and she was overcome by embarrassment. She hid her face in her hands. Dad stroked her back proudly. Annabelle pretended not to be interested, and helped herself to another stale crisp.

'She should really come out here and take a bow,' announced Mr Stink.

'No, no, no,' snapped Mother.

'No, Mrs Crumb,' said Sir David. 'I think we'd all like to meet this extraordinary little girl.'

The audience applauded his suggestion. But Chloe felt glued to her seat. She couldn't even speak out loud in front of the class. She didn't want to be on television in front of millions of people!

What would she say? What would she do? She didn't know any tricks. This was going to be the most embarrassing moment of her life, even worse than when she threw up her macaroni cheese all over Miss Spratt in the language lab. But the applause was getting louder and louder, and eventually Dad took her hand and gently pulled her to her feet.

'You're feeling shy, aren't you?' whispered Dad.

Chloe nodded.

'Well you shouldn't. You're a fantastic girl. You should be proud of what you've done. Now come on. Enjoy your moment in the limelight!'

Hand in hand they raced down the corridor towards the set. Just out of sight of the cameras

Dad let her hand go, and smiled supportively as she stepped out into the light. The audience applauded wildly. Mr Stink beamed over at her, and she tried to beam back. Mother was the only person not applauding, so Chloe's eyes were drawn towards her. Chloe tried to meet her gaze, but Mother turned her head sharply to look the other way. This made Chloe even more uncomfortable, and she tried to do a curtsy but didn't really know how to, and then ran off the stage, back into the safety of the stale crisps room.

'What a charming child,' said Sir David. He turned to Mother. 'Now I have to ask you, Mrs Crumb. Why did you lie? Was it purely to further your own political ambitions?'

The other guests from rival political parties looked at Mrs Crumb and tutted. As if *they* would ever dream of doing anything so immoral! Mother started to perspire. Her hair lacquer began to melt and her make-up ran slowly down her face. Dad, Chloe and Annabelle sat and watched her squirm, unable to help.

'Well, as if anyone would want that old tramp in their house,' she shouted finally. 'Look at him! You lot watching this at home can't smell him, but take it from me, he stinks! He stinks of dirt and sweat and poo and pond and dog. I wish that great stinky stinker would just stink off out of my home for ever!'

There was shocked silence for a moment. Then the boos started, getting louder and louder. Mother looked at the audience in panic. At that moment her bouffant collapsed.

18

RABBIT DROPPINGS

'WE WANT STINK! WE WANT STINK!'

Chloe peeked through a gap in the curtains. There was a huge crowd of people outside their house. News reporters, camera crews, and hundreds and hundreds of local people waving large pieces of cardboard emblazoned with slogans.

Mr Stink's appearance on television the previous night had obviously had an enormous effect on people. Overnight he had gone from being an unknown smelly tramp to a hugely famous smelly tramp.

Chloe put on her dressing gown and raced down to the shed.

'Is it time for Lily to meet the flesh-eating zombie teachers?' enquired Mr Stink as she entered.

'No, no, no, Mr Stink! Can't you hear the crowds outside?!'

'I'm sorry, I can't hear you properly,' he said. 'I found these rabbit droppings in the garden. They make excellent earplugs.' He popped out the two little brown pellets as Chloe looked on with a curious mixture of disgust and admiration at his ingenuity. For those of you who may find yourself out in the wild and in need of earplugs, just follow this easy step-by-step guide.

Fig A

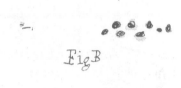

Fig B

First find a
friendly rabbit.

Wait patiently for it to
deposit some droppings
for you.

Fig C

Fig D

Insert one in each
ear. Larger ears
will require bigger
droppings and
possibly even a
bigger rabbit.

Enjoy a great night's
sleep only slightly
marred by the smell
of rabbit poo.

The Duchess sniffed at the droppings in the vain hope that they might be a couple of rogue Maltesers or at the very worst some of Raj's despised coffee Revels, but quickly turned up her nose when she realised they were poo, and went back to her makeshift basket.

'That's better,' said Mr Stink. 'You know, I had the strangest dream last night, Miss Chloe. I was on television discussing all the important issues of the day! Your mother was there too! It was hilarious!'

'That was no dream, Mr Stink. That really happened.'

'Oh, dear,' said the tramp. 'Maybe it wasn't so funny after all.'

'It was *hilarious*, Mr Stink. You were the star of the show. And now there's hundreds of people camped outside the house.'

'What on earth do they want, child?'

'You!' said Chloe. 'They want to interview you I think. And some people want you to be the Prime Minister!'

The crowd was getting louder and louder now. 'WE WANT STINK! WE WANT STINK! WE WANT STINK!'

'Oh my word, yes I can hear them. They want me as Prime Minister, you say? Ha ha! I must remember to appear on television more often! Maybe I can be king next too!'

'You'd better get up, Mr Stink. Now!'

'Yes, of course, Miss Chloe. Right, I want to look smart for my fans.'

He bumbled around the shed sniffing his clothes and grimacing. *If even he thinks they're smelly*, thought Chloe, *they must be really bad*.

'I could put some clothes on a quick wash and dry for you,' she offered hopefully.

'No, thank you, my dear. I don't think washing machines are hygienic. I'll just get the Duchess to chew some of the particularly nasty stains out.'

He dug through a pile of his clothes and pulled out a pair of spectacularly dirt-encrusted brown trousers. Whether they had been brown when they started their life was now anybody's guess. He passed them to the Duchess, who began her task of a reluctant dry cleaner and started munching on the stains.

Chloe cleared her throat. 'Um . . . Mr Stink. You said on the TV show how every homeless person has a different story to tell. Well, can you tell me your story? I mean, why did you end up on the streets?'

'Why do you think, my dear?'

'I don't know. I've got millions of theories. Maybe you were abandoned in a forest as a baby and raised by a pack of wolves?'

'No!' he chuckled.

'Or I reckon you were a world-famous rock star who faked your own death as you couldn't handle all the adulation.'

'I wish I was!'

'All right then, you were a top scientist who invented the most powerful bomb in the world and then, realising its dangers, went on the run from the military.'

'Well, those are all very imaginative guesses,' he said. 'But I am sorry, none of them are right. You're not even close, I'm afraid.'

'I thought not.'

'I will tell you when the time is right, Chloe.'

'Promise?'

'I promise. Now please give me a few minutes, my dear. I must get ready to greet my public!'

19

SUPERTRAMP

'I AM NOT APOLOGISING TO HIM!'

'YOU HAVE TO!'

Mr Stink sat at the head of the kitchen table reading all about himself in the newspapers as Chloe stood at the stove frying some sausages for him. Her parents were arguing again in the next room. It wasn't a conversation that their house guest was meant to hear, but they were so angry their voices were becoming louder and louder.

'BUT HE DOES SMELL!'

'I KNOW HE SMELLS BUT YOU DIDN'T NEED TO SAY IT ON THE TELEVISION.'

Chloe smiled over at Mr Stink. He looked so engrossed in all the headlines, 'Supertramp!', 'Stinky Superstar Steals Show!', 'Homeless Man Saves Boring Election', that he appeared not to be listening. Or maybe he'd put his rabbit dropping earplugs back in.

'OBVIOUSLY NOT!' shouted Mother. 'LAST NIGHT I HAD ANOTHER CALL FROM THE PRIME MINISTER TELLING ME I HAVE EMBARRASSED THE PARTY AND HE WANTS ME TO WITHDRAW AS A CANDIDATE!'

'GOOD!'

'WHAT DO YOU MEAN "GOOD"?!'

'THIS WHOLE THING HAS TURNED YOU INTO A MONSTER!' shouted Dad.

'WHAT?! I AM NOT A MONSTER!'

'YES, YOU ARE! MONSTER! MONSTER! MONSTER!'

'HOW DARE YOU?!' screamed Mother.

'GO AND APOLOGISE TO HIM!'

'NO!'

'APOLOGISE!'

For a moment all you could hear was the sizzle of sausage fat and lard in the frying pan. Then, slowly, the door opened and Mother oozed like slime into the room. Her bouffant was still not what it was. She hesitated for a moment. Her husband appeared in the doorway and gave her a stern look. She did a little theatrical cough.

'Her-hum. Mr Stink?' she ventured.

'Yes, Mrs Crumb?' replied Mr Stink without looking up, still engrossed in the papers.

'I would like to say . . . sorry.'

'What on earth for?' he enquired.

'For what I said about you on *Question Time* last night. About you smelling of all those things. It was impolite.'

'Thank you so much, Mrs . . .'

'Call me Janet.'

'Thank you so much, Mrs Janet. It *was* rather hurtful as I do pride myself on my personal hygiene. Indeed I had a bath just before I went on the show.'

'Well, you didn't really have a *bath*, did you? You had a *pond.*'

'Yes, I suppose you're right. I did have a pond. And if you so wish I will have another "pond" next year, so I remain perfectly clean.'

'But you're not clean you sti—' began Mother.

'Be nice!' interrupted Dad forcibly.

'You don't know this,' said Mother to Mr Stink.

'But after what I said on *Question Time* last night I have been asked by the Prime Minister to pull out of the election.'

'Yes, I do know actually. I heard you and your husband arguing just a moment ago in the living room.'

'Oh,' said Mother, uncharacteristically lost for words.

'Sausages are ready!' said Chloe, trying to save her Mother from further humiliation.

'I'd better be off to work now, love,' said Dad. 'I don't want to be late.'

'Yes, yes,' said Mother waving him away distractedly. He discreetly picked up a couple of slices of bread and slipped them in his pocket on the way out. Chloe heard the front door loudly open and close, and then the door to the room under the stairs very quietly do the same.

'Just seven sausages today please, Miss Chloe,' said Mr Stink. 'I don't want to put on weight. I have to think of my fan base.'

'Fan base?!' said Mother in a barely disguised jealous rage.

The telephone, which had been crouching on the table doing very little, suddenly sang its little song. Chloe picked it up. 'Crooombe residence. Who is speaking please . . .? It's the Prime Minister!'

Mother's face lit up with hope, and even her bouffant seemed to perk up a bit. 'Ah yes! I knew my darling Dave would change his mind!'

115

'He wants to talk to Mr Stink, actually,' continued Chloe. Mother's smile turned upside down.

Mr Stink picked up the receiver with a nonchalance that suggested he often received calls from world leaders. 'Stink here. Yes? Yes? Oh yes . . . ?'

Mum and Chloe studied his face like a map, trying to read from his reactions what the Prime Minister was saying.

'Yes, yes, yes. Well, yes, thank you Prime Minister.'

Mr Stink put the receiver down and sat back at the table to resume his now daily task of reading about himself in the newspapers.

'*Well*?' asked Chloe.

'Yes, well?' chimed in Mother.

'The Prime Minister has invited me to go for tea at Number Ten Downing Street today,' said Mr Stink matter-of-factly. 'He wants me to take over from you, Mrs Crumb, as the local candidate. May I have those sausages now please, Chloe?'

20

GRUBBY TOILET ROLL

'Hoooorrraaaayyyyy!' There was a huge cheer as Mr Stink appeared at the upstairs window. All he had to do was stand and wave for the crowd to roar their approval. The cameras all zoomed in and the microphones leaned forward. One lady even held her baby up so the infant could catch sight of this new star. Chloe stood a few paces behind Mr Stink, watching like a proud parent. She hadn't enjoyed being on the television that much and preferred to let Mr Stink take centre stage. He gestured for everyone to be quiet. And there was quiet.

'I have written a short speech,' he announced, before unrolling a very long, grubby toilet roll and reading from it.

'First of all, may I say how very honoured I am that you have all turned out to see me

today.'

The crowd cheered again.

'I am but a humble wanderer. A vagrant maybe, certainly a vagabond, a street dreamer if you will . . .'

'Oh, get on with it!' hissed Mother from behind Chloe.

'Shussshh!' shushed Chloe.

'As such, I had no idea that simply appearing on the electric televisual apparatus would have quite such an astonishing effect. All I can say at this time is that I am meeting with the Prime Minister today at Number Ten to discuss my political future.'

The crowd went wild.

'Thank you all for your incredible kindness,' he concluded, before rolling his toilet roll back up and disappearing from view.

'Miss Chloe?' he said.

'Yes?' she answered.

'If I am meeting the Prime Minister I think I need a make over.'

Chloe wasn't sure exactly what a 'make over' was. She knew there were lots of shows on TV that did make overs, but Mother didn't allow her to watch them. Feeling like the ugly duckling of the family she didn't own any make-up either, so tentatively she knocked on her little sister's door to see if she could borrow some. Annabelle had drawers full of make-up. She always asked for it for her birthday and Christmas, as she liked

118

nothing better than painting it all on and performing her own little beauty pageants in front of her bedroom mirror.

'Has he gone yet?' asked Annabelle.

'No, he hasn't. Maybe if you bothered to talk to him you would see how nice he is.'

'He smells.'

'So do you,' said Chloe. 'Now, I need to borrow some of your make-up.'

'Why? You don't wear make-up. You're not pretty, so there's no point.'

For a moment Chloe entertained a number of fantasies where her little sister met horrific ends. Plunged into a pool of piranhas perhaps? Abandoned in the Arctic wastes in her underwear? Force-fed marshmallows until she exploded?

'It's for Mr Stink,' she said, filing away all those fantasies in her brain for a later date.

'No way.'

'I'll tell Mother you're the one who's been secretly scoffing her Bendicks chocolate mints.'

'What do you need?' replied Annabelle in a heartbeat.

*   *   *

Later, Mr Stink sat on an upturned plant pot in the shed as the two girls fussed around him.

'It's not too much, is it?' he enquired.

Unexpectedly enjoying herself, Annabelle had gone a little over the top. Did Mr Stink really need pink glittery blusher, electric-blue eyeliner, purple eye shadow and orange nail varnish to go and meet the Prime Minister?

'Erm . . .' said Chloe.

119

'No, you look great, Mr Stink!' said Annabelle, as she attached a butterfly hair-clip to his head. 'This is so much fun! It's the best Christmas Eve ever!'

'Aren't you supposed to be singing carols in church or something?' asked Chloe knowingly.

'Yes, but I hate it. It's so boring. This is way more cool.' Annabelle looked thoughtful. 'You know, it's so tedious sometimes doing all those stupid hobbies and sports and stuff.'

'Why do them then?' enquired Chloe.

'Yes, why do them, dear?' chimed in Mr Stink.

Annabelle looked confused. 'I don't know really. I suppose to make Mother happy,' she said.

'Your Mother won't be truly happy if you aren't. You need to find the things that make *you* happy,' said Mr Stink with authority. It was hard to take him seriously though, what with his multi-coloured eye make-up.

'Well . . . this afternoon has made me happy,' said Annabelle. She smiled at Chloe for the first time in years. 'Hanging out with *you* has made me happy.'

Chloe smiled back, and they nervously held each other's gaze for a moment.

'What about me?' demanded Mr Stink.

'You too of course!' laughed Annabelle. 'You actually get used to the smell after a while,' she whispered to Chloe, who shushed her and smiled.

All of a sudden the shed shook violently. Chloe rushed to the door and opened it to see a helicopter hovering overhead. Engine whirring, it slowly came down to land in their garden.

'Ah, yes. The Prime Minister said he would be sending that to pick us up,' announced Mr Stink.

'Us?' said Chloe.

'You don't think I was going to go without you, do you?'

21

WET WIPE

'Why don't you come too?' shouted Chloe to Annabelle over the thunderous noise of the blades.

'No, this is your day, Chloe,' her little sister hollered back. 'This is all because of you. And besides, that helicopter's tiny. It'll absolutely *whiff* in there . . .'

Chloe grinned and waved goodbye as the helicopter slowly ascended, flattening most of the plants and flowers in the garden as it did so. Mother's bouffant danced around her head like candyfloss on a windy day at the seafront as she attempted to hold it down. Elizabeth the cat got blown across the lawn. She tried desperately to cling on to the grass with her claws. But despite meowing for mercy the wind from the blades was just too strong and she shot across the garden like a furry cannonball and into the pond.

Plop!

The Duchess looked down from the helicopter window, smirking.

As they glided up and up and up Chloe saw her house, and her street, and her town get smaller and smaller. Soon the postal districts were packed below her like squares on a chessboard. It was unutterably thrilling. For the first time in her life, Chloe felt like she was at the centre of the world. She looked over at Mr Stink. He was getting re-acquainted with a toffee bon-bon that, from the looks of it, had been in his trouser pocket since the late 1950s. Apart from his jaw working desperately to chew the ancient confectionery he looked perfectly relaxed, as if taking a helicopter ride to see the Prime Minister was something he did most days.

Chloe smiled over at him, and he smiled back with that special twinkle in his eye that almost made you forget how bad he smelled.

Mr Stink tapped on the pilot's shoulder. 'Are you going to be coming round with a trolley service at any point?' he asked.

'It's just a short flight, sir.'

'Any chance of a cup of tea and a bun then?'

'I am very sorry, sir,' replied the pilot with a firmness that suggested this conversation was about to be over.

'Very disappointing,' said Mr Stink.

Chloe recognised the door of Number Ten Downing Street, because it was always on those boring political shows she was allowed to watch on Sunday mornings. It was big and black and always had a policeman standing outside. She thought, *If I joined the police I would want to be chasing baddies all day, not standing outside a door thinking about whether or not I should have spaghetti hoops for my tea.* However, she wisely kept that thought to herself as the policeman opened the door for them with a smile.

*   *   *

'Please take a seat,' said an immaculately dressed butler haughtily. The staff were used to playing host to royalty and world leaders at 10 Downing Street, not a little girl, a transvestite tramp and his dog. 'The Prime Minister will be with you shortly.'

They were standing in a big oak-panelled room with dozens of gold-framed oil paintings of serious-looking old men staring out at you from the walls. The tinsel round the frames did little to counter their severe looks. Suddenly, the double doors flew open and a herd of men in suits approached them.

'Good afternoon, Mr Stinky!' said the Prime Minister. You could tell he was in charge as he was walking at the front of the herd.

'It's just Stink, Prime Minister,' corrected one of his advisors.

'How are you doing, mate?' said the Prime Minister, trying to downplay his poshness. He offered out his perfectly manicured and moisturized little hand for Mr Stink to shake. The tramp offered his own big dirty gnarled hand and, looking at it, the Prime Minister quickly withdrew his, preferring to give his new best friend a mock punch on the shoulder. He then examined his knuckles and noticed they had some grime on them.

'Wet wipe!' he demanded. 'Now!'

A man at the back of the herd hurriedly produced a wet wipe and it was passed forward to the Prime Minister. He quickly wiped his hand with it before passing it back to the man at the back.

'A pleasure to meet you too, Mr Prime Minister,' said Mr Stink without conviction.

'Call me Dave,' said the Prime Minister. 'Gosh, he does smell like a toilet,' he whispered to one of his advisors.

Mr Stink looked at Chloe, hurt, but the Prime

Minister didn't notice. 'So, you made quite a splash on *Question Time*, my homeless pal,' he continued. 'Ruddy hilarious. Ha ha ha!' He wiped away a non-existent tear of laughter from his eye. 'I think we could use you.'

'*Use* him?' asked Chloe suspiciously.

'Yeah, yeah. It's no secret it's not looking good for me in the election. My approval rating with the public right now is . . .'

One of the herd hastily opened a folder and there was a long pause as he flicked through pages and pages of information.

'Bad.'

'Bad. Right. *Thanks*, Perkins,' said the Prime Minister, sarcastically.

'It's Brownlow.'

'Whatever.' The Prime Minister turned back to Mr Stink. 'I think if we had you, a real life tramp, take over from Mrs Crumb as candidate it could be brilliant. It's far too late to rope anyone else in now, and you would be the ideal last-minute replacement. You're just so *funny*. I mean, to laugh *at*, not really with.'

'Excuse me?' said Chloe, feeling very protective of her friend now.

The Prime Minister ignored her. 'It's genius! It really is. If you joined the party it would fool the public into thinking we *cared* about the homeless! Maybe one day I could even make you Minister for Soap-Dodgers.'

'Soap-Dodgers?' said Mr Stink.

'Yeah, you know, the homeless.'

'Right,' said Mr Stink. 'And as Minister for the Homeless, I would be able to help other homeless people?'

'Well, no,' said the Prime Minister. 'It wouldn't *mean* anything, just make me look like a fantastic tramp-loving guy. Well, wadda you say, Mr Stinky-poo?'

Mr Stink looked very ill at ease. 'I don't . . . I mean . . . I'm not sure—'

'Are you *kidding* me?' laughed the Prime Minister. 'You're a tramp! You can't have anything better to do!'

The suited herd laughed too. Suddenly Chloe had a flashback to her school. The Prime Minister and his aides were behaving exactly like the gang of mean girls in her year. Still stumbling for words, Mr Stink looked over to her for help.

'Prime Minister . . . ?' said Chloe.

'Yes?' he answered with an expectant smile.

'Why don't you stick it up your fat bum!'

'You took the words right out of my mouth, child!' chuckled Mr Stink. 'Goodbye, Prime Minister, and Merry Christmas to you all!'

22

LONG LION DAYS

Chloe and Mr Stink weren't invited to take the helicopter home. They had to get the bus.

As it was Christmas Eve, the bus was chock-a-block with people, most of them barely visible under their mountains of shopping bags. As Chloe and Mr Stink sat side by side on the top deck, bare branches dragged against the grimy windows.

'Did you see the look on his face when you told him to stick it up his . . . ?' exclaimed Mr Stink.

'I can't believe I did it!' said Chloe.

'I'm so glad you did,' said Mr Stink. 'Thank you so much for sticking up for me.'

'Well, you stuck up for me with that awful Rosamund!'

' "Stick it up your bum!" ' So naughty! Though I might have said something far ruder! Ha ha!'

They laughed together. Mr Stink reached into his trouser pocket to pull out a dirty old handkerchief to dry his tears of joy. As he raised the handkerchief to his face, Chloe spotted that a label had been sewn on to it. Peering closer, she saw that the label was made of silk, and a name was embroidered delicately on it . . .

'Lord . . . Darlington?' she read.

There was silence for a moment.

'Is that *you*?' said Chloe. 'Are you a lord?'

'No . . . no . . .' said Mr Stink. 'I'm just a humble vagabond. I got this handkerchief . . . from a jumble sale.'

'May I see your silver spoon then?' said Chloe, gently.

Mr Stink gave a resigned smile. He reached into his jacket pocket and slowly withdrew the spoon, then handed it to her. Chloe turned it over in her hands. Looking at it close up, she realised she'd been wrong. It wasn't three letters engraved on it. It was a single letter on a crest, held on each side by a lion.

A single, capital letter D.

'You *are* Lord Darlington,' said Chloe. 'Let me see that old photograph again.'

Mr Stink carefully pulled out his old black and white photograph.

Chloe studied it for a few seconds. It was just as she'd remembered. The beautiful young couple, the Rolls-Royce, the stately home. Only now, when she looked at it, she could see the resemblance between the young man in the photo and the old tramp beside her. 'And that's you in the picture.'

Chloe held the photograph delicately, knowing she was handling something very precious. Mr Stink looked much younger, especially without his beard and dirt. But the eyes were sparkling. It was

129

unmistakably him.

'The game's up,' said Mr Stink. 'That *is* me, Chloe. A lifetime ago.'

'And who's this lady with you?'

'My wife.'

'Your wife? I didn't know you were married.'

'You didn't know I was a lord, either,' said Mr Stink.

'And that must be your house then, Lord Darlington,' said Chloe, indicating the stately home standing behind the couple in the photograph. Mr Stink nodded. 'Well then, how come you're homeless now?'

'It's a long story, my dear,' said Mr Stink, evasively.

'But I want to hear it,' said Chloe. 'Please? I've told you so much about my life. And I've always wanted to know your story, Mr Stink, ever since I first saw you. I always knew you must have a fascinating tale to tell.'

Mr Stink took a breath. 'Well, I had it all, child. More money than I could ever spend, a beautiful house with its own lake. My life was like an endless summer. Croquet, tea on the lawn, long lion days spent playing cricket. And to make things even more perfect I married this beautiful, clever, funny, adorable woman, my childhood sweetheart. Violet.'

'She is beautiful.'

'Yes, yes, she is. She was. Unutterably so. We were deliriously happy, you know.'

It was all so obvious now to Chloe. The way Mr Stink had expertly bowled the screwed up piece of paper into the bin, his silver monogrammed cutlery and his impeccable table manners, his insistence on walking on the outside of the pavement, the way he had decorated the shed. It was all true. He was *super*-posh.

'Soon after that photograph was taken Violet became pregnant,' continued Mr Stink. 'I couldn't have been more thrilled. But one night, when my wife was eight months pregnant, my chauffeur drove me to London to have dinner with a group of my old school friends at a gentlemen's club. It was just before Christmas, actually. I stayed late into the night, selfishly drinking and talking and smoking cigars . . .'

'What do you mean, selfishly?' said Chloe.

'Because I should never have gone. We were caught in a blizzard on the way home. I didn't get back until just before dawn, and found that the house was ablaze . . .'

'Oh no!' cried Chloe, not sure if she could bear to hear the rest of the story.

'A piece of coal must have fallen out of the fireplace in our bedroom, and set the carpet alight as she slept. I ran out of the Rolls and waded through the deep snow. Desperately I tried to fight my way into the house, but the fire brigade wouldn't let me. It took five of them to hold me back. They tried their best to save her but it was too late. The roof fell in. Violet didn't stand a chance.'

'Oh my God!' Chloe gasped.

Tears filled the old tramp's eyes. Chloe didn't know what to do. Dealing with emotions was a new thing to her, but tentatively she reached out her hand to comfort him. Time seemed to slow down as her hand reached his. This made the tears really flow, and he shook with half a century of pain.

'If only I hadn't been at the club that night, I could have saved her. I could have held her all night, made her feel safe and warm. She wouldn't have needed the fire. My darling, darling Violet.' Chloe squeezed his dirty hand tight.

'You can't blame yourself for the fire.'

'I should have been there for her. I should have been there . . .'

'It was an accident,' said Chloe. 'You have to forgive yourself.'

'I can't. I never can.'

'You are a good man, Mr Stink. What happened was a terrible accident. You must believe that.'

'Thank you, child. I shouldn't really cry. Not on public transport.' He sniffed, and gathered himself together a little.

'So,' said Chloe, 'how you did you end up living on the streets?'

'Well, I was heartbroken. Utterly inconsolable. I had lost my unborn child and the woman I loved. After the funeral I tried to return to the house. Lived alone in a wing that hadn't been so badly damaged by the blaze. But the house carried so many painful memories, I couldn't sleep. Being there gave me terrible nightmares. I kept seeing her face in the flames. I had to get away. So one day I started walking and I never came back.'

'I am so sorry,' said Chloe. 'If people only knew that . . .'

'Like I said on the televisual apparatus, every homeless person has a story to tell,' said Mr Stink. 'That's mine. I am sorry it didn't involve spies or pirates or what have you. Real life isn't like that, I'm afraid. And I didn't mean to upset you.'

'Christmas must be the hardest time for you,'

said Chloe.

'Yes, yes, of course. Christmas is an emblem of perfect happiness I find very hard to bear. It's a time when families come together. For me it's a reminder of who's not there.'

The bus reached their stop, and Chloe's arm found a home in Mr Stink's as they walked towards the family house. She was relieved to see that all the reporters and camera crews had moved on. The funny old tramp must be old news by now.

'I just wish I could make everything right,' said Chloe.

'But you are making everything right, Miss Chloe. Ever since you came and talked to me. You've made me smile again. You've been so kind to me. You know, if my child had ended up like you, I would have been very proud.'

Chloe was so touched she could hardly think what to say. 'Well,' she said, 'I know you would have made a great dad.'

'Thank you, child. Unimaginable kindness.'

Nearing the house, Chloe looked at it and realised something. She didn't *want* to go home. She didn't want to live with her awful Mother and have to go to that horrible posh school any more. They walked in silence for a moment, then Chloe took a deep breath and turned to Mr Stink.

'I don't want to go back there,' she said. 'I want to go wandering with you.'

PLASTIC SNOWMAN

'I'm sorry Miss Chloe, but you can't possibly come with me,' said Mr Stink as they stood in the driveway.

'Why not?' protested Chloe.

'For a million different reasons!'

'Name one!'

'It's too cold.'

'I don't mind the cold.'

'Well,' said Mr Stink, 'living on the streets is far too dangerous for a young girl like you.'

'I'm nearly thirteen!'

'It's very important you don't miss school.'

'I hate school,' said Chloe. 'Please please please, Mr Stink. Let me come with you and the Duchess. I want to be a wanderer like you.'

'You must think about this properly for a moment, child,' said Mr Stink. 'What on earth is your mother going to say?'

'I don't care,' snapped Chloe. 'I hate her anyway.'

'I've told you before, you mustn't say that.'

'But it's true.'

Mr Stink sighed. 'Your mind is made up is it?'

'One hundred percent!'

'Well, in that case, I'd better go and talk to your mother for you.'

Chloe grinned. This was superbrilliantamazing! It was really going to happen. She was going to be free at last! No more being sent to bed early. No more maths homework. No more wearing yellow frilly dresses that made her look like a Quality Street. Chloe was a hundred times more excited than she had ever been in her life. She and Mr Stink were going to wander the world together, eating sausages for breakfast, lunch and dinner, having baths in ponds, and emptying Starbucks wherever they went . . .

'Thanks so much, Mr Stink,' she said, as she put her key in the lock for the last time.

*   *   *

As Chloe raced excitedly around her room throwing clothes and the chocolate bars she had hidden under her bed into her bag, she could hear faint voices in the kitchen downstairs. Mother won't care, thought Chloe. She'll hardly miss me anyway! The only person she cares about is Annabelle.

Chloe looked around her little pink room. Strangely, she felt a tingle of fondness for it now that she was leaving. And she was going to miss Dad, and of course Annabelle, and even Elizabeth the cat, but a new life was calling her. A life of mystery and adventure. A life of making up bedtime stories about vampires and zombies. A life of burping in the faces of bullies!

Just then, there was a gentle knock on the door. 'I'm just coming, Mr Stink!' Chloe called out, as she threw the last ornamental owl into her bag.

The door opened slowly. Chloe turned around and gasped.

It wasn't Mr Stink.

It was Mother. She stood in the corridor, her

eyes red from crying. A tear was running down her cheek and a little plastic snowman dangled incongruously above her head.

'My darling Chloe,' she spluttered. 'Mr Stink just told me you wanted to leave home. Please. I beg you, don't go.'

Chloe had never seen Mother looking so sad. Suddenly, she felt a little guilty. 'I, er, just thought you wouldn't mind,' she said.

'Mind? I couldn't bear it if you left.' Mother started sobbing now. This was so unlike her. It was as if Chloe was looking at another person entirely.

'What did Mr Stink say to you?' she asked.

'The old man gave me a good talking to,' said Mother. 'Said how unhappy you've been at home. How I had to work at being a better mother. He told me how he'd lost his own family, and if I wasn't careful, I was going to lose you. I felt so ashamed. I know we haven't always seen eye to eye on things Chloe, but I do love you. I really do.'

Chloe was horrified. She'd thought Mr Stink was just going to ask if she could go with him, but instead he'd made Mother cry. She was furious with him. This wasn't the plan at all!

And just then, Mr Stink appeared solemnly in the doorway. He stood a pace behind Mother.

'I'm sorry Chloe,' he ventured. 'I hope you can forgive me.'

'Why did you say what you did?' she asked angrily. 'I thought we were going to wander the world together.'

Mr Stink smiled kindly. 'Maybe one day you'll wander the world on your own,' he said. 'But for now, trust me, you need your family. I would give anything to have mine back. Anything.'

Mother's legs looked like they were going to give way, and she stumbled towards Chloe's bed. She sat there and wept, hiding her face in shame at her tears. Chloe looked at Mr Stink silently for a long time. Deep down, she knew he was right.

'Of course I forgive you,' she said to him finally, and he smiled that eye-twinkling smile of his.

Then she softly sat down next to her mother and put an arm around her.

'And I love you too, Mum. Very much.'

24

YUCKETY YUCK YUCK

It was well into the night on Christmas Eve now, and down in the living room, Dad waved a large festive assortment tin under Mr Stink's nose. 'Would you like a biscuit?' he asked.

Dad had already scoffed quite a few, having been hiding in the room under the stairs again all day with only a couple of slices of dry bread to keep him going. Mr Stink eyed the contents of the tin with disgust.

'Have you any stale ones?' he asked. 'Maybe with just a hint of mould?'

'I don't think so, sorry,' replied Dad.

'No thank you then,' said Mr Stink. He patted the Duchess, who was sitting on his lap, trading evil looks across the coffee table with Elizabeth. The family cat was bundled up in a towel on Annabelle's lap, still recovering from her 'swim'.

'Never mind about the biscuits,' said Annabelle. 'I want to know what you said to the Prime Minister's offer?'

'Chloe told him to stick it up his—'

'We told him he wasn't interested,' interjected Chloe hastily. 'So maybe you can still stand to be the local MP, Mum.'

'Oh no, I don't want to,' said Mum. 'Not after I humiliated myself on television.'

'But now you've met Mr Stink and seen how other people live their lives you could try to make things *better* for people,' suggested Chloe.

'Well, perhaps I could try and stand again at the next election,' said Mother. 'Though I will have to change my policies. Especially the one about the homeless. I am sorry I got it so wrong.'

'And the one about the unemployed, eh, Dad?' said Chloe.

'What's this?' said Mother.

'Thank you, Chloe,' said Dad sarcastically. 'Well, I didn't want to tell you, but the car factory looks like it's going to close soon and it had to let most of us go.'

'So you are . . . ?' asked Mother incredulous.

'Unemployed, yes. Or "dole scum" as you might say. I was too scared to tell you so I've been hiding in the room under the stairs for the last month.'

'What do you mean, you were too scared to tell me? I love you, and I always will, whether you've got a job at the stupid car factory or not.'

Dad put his arm around her and she nuzzled up her head to meet his lips with hers. Their kiss lingered for a few moments, as Chloe and Annabelle looked on with a mixture of pride and embarrassment. Your parents kissing. Nice but somehow yuck. Them snogging is even worse. Yuckety yuck yuck.

'I *would* go back to being in a rock band, but you put my guitar on the bonfire!' said Dad with a chuckle.

'Don't!' said Mum. 'I still feel so bad about that. I fell for you like a ton of bricks when I first saw you on stage with the band. That's why I married you. But when the album didn't sell I could see how upset you were, and I couldn't bear it. I thought I was trying to help you move on with your life, but now I realise all I did was crush your dreams. And that's why I don't want to make the same mistake twice.'

She got up and started searching in the bottom drawer of the sideboard where she kept her secret stash of Bendicks chocolate mints. 'I am so sorry I tore up your story, Chloe.' Mum pulled out the maths exercise book of Chloe's that she had ripped to pieces. She had painstakingly sellotaped the whole thing back together, and her eyes still shining with tears she handed it back to Chloe. 'After *Question Time* I had a lot of time to think,' she said. 'I fished this out of the bin and I read it to the end, Chloe. It's brilliant.'

Chloe took back the book with a smile. 'I promise to try harder in my maths lessons from now on, Mum.'

'Thank you, Chloe. And I have something for you too, my darling,' said Mum to Dad. From under the tree she pulled out a beautifully wrapped present that was exactly the shape of an electric guitar.

25

BLACK LEATHER MISTLETOE

'I've got some black leather mistletoe this Christmas,
  I'm gonna kiss you and give you a bad shaving rash . . .'

Dad had plugged his shiny new electric guitar into its amp and was strutting up and down the living room exuberantly singing one of his old band's songs. He was clearly having the time of his life. It was almost as if his perm had grown back too. Mum, Chloe, Annabelle and Mr Stink sat on the sofa and clapped along. Even Elizabeth and the Duchess were curled up together nodding their heads in time with the music. The heavy rock wasn't quite to Mr Stink's taste, and to combat the noise he had discreetly re-inserted his rabbit-dropping earplugs.

  'Yeah baby I'm gonna feast on your mince pies,
  And give you a real good yuletide surprise . . . !'

The song ended with a huge flourish on Dad's guitar, and his tiny stadium of fans cheered and clapped him excitedly.

'Thank you, Wembley. Thank you so much. That was, of course, The Serpents of Doom's Christmas single, "Black Leather Mistletoe", which rocketed to number 98 in the charts. Now for my next song . . .'

'I think that's enough heavy rock music just for now, dear,' said Mum, as if she might already be regretting giving him that present. She turned to Chloe and said, 'You don't want to leave any more, do you?'

'No Mum, not in a million years. This is the best Christmas ever.'

'Oh, wonderful!' said Mum. 'It's super that we are all together having fun like this.'

'But . . .' said Chloe. 'There is one thing I would like.'

'Name it,' said Mum.

'I would like Mr Stink to move in properly.'

'What?' asked Mum with a gasp.

'That's a great idea,' said Dad. 'We've all loved

having you around, Mr Stink.'

'Yes, you feel like part of the family now,' said Annabelle.

'Well, I suppose he could stay for a little while longer in the shed . . .' said Mum reluctantly.

'I didn't mean in the shed. I meant in our house,' said Chloe.

'Of course,' said Dad.

'That would be great!' chimed in Annabelle.

'Well, erm, oh, um . . .' Mum looked increasingly flustered. 'I do really appreciate what Mr Stink has done for us, but I'm not sure he would feel at home here. I don't imagine he has ever lived in a house as nice as this . . .'

'Actually, Mr Stink used to live in a stately home,' corrected Chloe gleefully.

'What? As a servant?' said Mum.

'No, it was *his* stately home. Mr Stink is really a lord.'

'A lord? Is this true, Mr Stink?'

'Yes, Mrs Crooooooombe.'

'A stately hobo! Well, that changes everything!' announced Mum, beaming with pride that she finally had someone truly posh in the house. 'Husband, take the plastic covers off the sofa. Annabelle, get out the best china! And if you would like to use the downstairs lavatory at any time Lord Stink, I have the key right here.'

'Thank you, but I don't need to go right now. Oh, hang on a moment . . .'

They all looked at Mr Stink expectantly. Chloe, Annabelle and Dad were just curious to finally see what the downstairs loo actually looked like from the inside, since none of them had ever been allowed in there.

'No . . . no, false alarm.'

Mum continued babbling breathlessly. 'And . . . and . . . and you can have our bedroom, your lordship! I can sleep on the sofa bed and my husband would be more than happy to move into the shed.'

'What the—?' said Dad.

'Please . . . please . . . please stay here with us,' interjected Chloe.

Mr Stink sat in silence for a moment. The cup and saucer in his hands started rattling, then a little tear formed in his eye. It travelled slowly down his cheek, creating a little streak of white on his grimy face. The Duchess looked up at him and tenderly licked it off her master's face. Chloe's hand tiptoed its way across the sofa to comfort him.

He held it tight. He held it so tight that she knew this was goodbye.

'Such unimaginable kindness. Thank you. Thank you all, so much. However, I am going to have to say no.'

'Stay with us for Christmas Day and Boxing Day at least,' pleaded Annabelle. 'Please . . .?' said Chloe.

'Thank you,' said Mr Stink. 'But I am afraid I have to refuse.'

'But why?' demanded Chloe.

'My work here is done. And I'm a wanderer,' said Mr Stink. 'It's time for me to wander on.'

'But we want you to be safe and warm here with us,' said Chloe. Tears were rolling down her cheeks now. Annabelle wiped away her sister's tears with her sleeve.

'I am sorry, Miss Chloe. I have to go. No tears

please. No fuss. Farewell to you all and thank you for all your kindness.' Mr Stink put down his cup and saucer, and headed for the door. 'Come on, Duchess,' he said. 'It's time to go.'

26

LITTLE STAR

He walked off into the moonlight. The moon was full and bright that night, and it looked so perfect that it couldn't be real. It was as if it had been painted, and hung there on a hook, it was so impossibly beautiful. There wasn't any snow, there never is at Christmas these days, except on the cards. Instead the streets were damp from a storm, and the moon was reflected in hundreds of little puddles. Most of the houses were adorned with Christmas decorations of one sort or another, with fairy-lit trees glinting through the double-glazing. The decorations looked almost beautiful too, competing with the moon and the stars in their own feeble way. All you could hear was the rhythmic scuff of Mr Stink's battered brogues as he walked slowly along the road, the Duchess following dutifully a pace behind, her head bowed.

Chloe watched him unseen from an upstairs window. Her hand touched the cold glass, trying to reach out to him. She watched him disappear out of sight, before sloping back to her room.

Then, sitting there on her bed, she remembered a reason to see him one last time.

'*Lily and the Flesh-Eating Zombie Teachers*!' she shouted, as she ran down the street.

'Miss Chloe?' said Mr Stink turning round.

'I have been thinking and thinking about Lily's second adventure. I would love to tell it to you now!'

'Write it down for me, child.'

'Write it down?' asked Chloe.

'Yes,' said Mr Stink. 'One day I want to walk into a bookshop and see your name on one of the covers. You have a talent for telling stories, Chloe.'

'*Do* I?' Chloe had never felt she had a talent for anything.

'Yes. All that time spent alone in your room will pay off one day. You have an extraordinary imagination, young lady. A real gift. You should share it with the world.'

'Thank you, Mr Stink,' said Chloe shyly.

'I'm glad you came running after me though,' said Mr Stink. 'I just remembered I have something for you.'

'For me?'

'Yes, I saved up all my loose change and bought you a Christmas present. I think it's something rather special.'

Mr Stink rummaged in his bag and pulled out a package wrapped in brown paper and tied up with string. He handed it to Chloe, who unwrapped it excitedly. Inside was a Teenage Mutant Ninja Turtles stationery set.

'It is a Teenybopper Mucus Karate Tortoise thing. I thought you'd like it. Mr Raj told me it was the very last one he had in his shop.'

'Did he now?' Chloe smiled. 'This is the best present I have ever had.' She wasn't lying. That Mr Stink had saved up all his pennies to buy her something meant the whole world to her. 'I will treasure this for ever, I promise.'

'Thank you,' said Mr Stink.

'And you've just given my whole family the best Christmas present ever. You brought us together.'

'Well, I'm not sure I can take all the credit for that!' he smiled. 'Now, you should really go home now, young Chloe. It's cold, and it feels like it's going to rain.'

'I don't like the thought of you sleeping outside,' she said. 'Especially on a cold damp night like this.'

Mr Stink smiled. 'I like being outside, you know. On our wedding night my darling Violet showed me the brightest star in the sky. Do you see? That one there?'

He pointed it out. It twinkled brightly like his eyes.

'I see it,' said Chloe.

'Well, that night we stood on the balcony of our bedroom and she said she would love me for as long as that star kept shining. So every night, before I go to sleep, I like to gaze at that star and think about her, and the great love we shared. I see the star, and it's her I see.'

'That's beautiful,' said Chloe, trembling and trying hard not to cry.

'My wife isn't gone. Every night she meets me in my dreams. Now go home. And don't worry about me, Miss Chloe. I have the Duchess and my star.'

'But I'll miss you,' said Chloe.

Mr Stink smiled, then pointed up at the sky. 'Do you see Violet's star?' he asked.

Chloe nodded.

'Do you see how there's another little star just under it?'

'Yes,' said Chloe. Up in the night sky, Violet's star burned brightly. Below it a smaller star twinkled in the blackness.

'Well, you are a very special young lady,' said

149

Mr Stink. 'And when I look at *that* star I am going to think about you.'

Chloe felt overwhelmed. 'Thank you,' she said. 'And I'll look at it and think about you.'

She gave him a big hug and didn't want to let go. He stood still and held her for a moment before rocking a little to set himself free. 'I have to go now. My soul is restless and I need to wander. Goodbye, Miss Chloe.'

'Goodbye, Mr Stink.'

The wanderer wandered off down the road as night slinked like a panther down the sky. She watched him disappear out of sight, until all that could be heard was silence echoing around the streets.

*   *   *

Later that night, Chloe sat alone on her bed. Mr Stink was gone. Perhaps for ever. But she could still smell him. She would always be able to smell him.

She opened her maths exercise book and began to write the first words of her new story.

Mr Stink stank . . .